La Vita Nuova

LA VITA NUOVA

DOVER THRIFT EDITIONS

Dante Alighieri

Translated by
Dante Gabriel Rossetti

DOVER PUBLICATIONS, INC.
MINEOLA, NEW YORK

DOVER THRIFT EDITIONS

GENERAL EDITOR: PAUL NEGRI

EDITOR OF THIS VOLUME: JOSLYN PINE

Copyright

Note copyright © 2001 by Dover Publications, Inc.
All rights reserved.

Bibliographical Note

This Dover edition, first published in 2001, is an unabridged republication of
Rossetti's translation of Dante's *La Vita Nuova*, which originally appeared in *The Early
Italian Poets from Ciullo d'Alcamo to Dante Alighieri (1100–1200–1300): in the original
metres, together with Dante's Vita Nuova*, translated by D. G. Rossetti, and published in
1861 by Smith & Elder, London. A new introductory Note has been specially prepared
for this edition.

Library of Congress Cataloging-in-Publication Data

Dante Alighieri, 1265–1321.
   [Vita nuova. English]
   La vita nuova / Dante Alighieri ; translated by Dante Gabriel Rossetti.
     p. cm.
   Originally published: London : Smith & Elder, 1861.
   ISBN-13: 978-0-486-41915-2
   ISBN-10: 0-486-41915-0 (pbk.)
   1. Rossetti, Dante Gabriel, 1828–1882. II. Title.

PQ4315.58 .R713 2001
851'.1—dc21

2001028585

Manufactured in the United States by LSC Communications
41915007   2020
www.doverpublications.com

Note

DANTE ALIGHIERI (1265–1321) is widely acknowledged as the greatest of Italian poets, occupying one of the three most honored places in Western literature, alongside Shakespeare and Goethe. He was born in Florence, Italy, at a propitious time in the city's history when trade and industry were flourishing. Although his family was descended from the feudal nobility, like many others of their class they were impoverished and losing ground to the new bourgeoisie. These circumstances did not adversely affect young Dante's education, however, since he completed primary school and continued with a course of study that included Latin, mathematics, and music—to which he formed a passionate attachment. And finally, like many Florentine intellectuals of his day, he learned to write verse. The diligent student grew into a learned scholar, an innovative political thinker, and the poet-visionary who would pen the epic poem *La Divina Commedia—The Divine Comedy*. As one critic described him, "Dante is not, as Homer is, the father of poetry springing in the freshness and simplicity of childhood out of the arms of mother earth; he is rather, like Noah, the father of a second poetical world, to whom he pours forth his prophetic song fraught with the wisdom and the experience of the old world."

Since not much is known of Dante's life—outside of what can be gleaned from his writings—it is illuminating to see him through the eyes of contemporaries who impart a sense of the man, and something of the depth and breadth of his accomplishments. A friend and neighbor, also a chronicler of the time, wrote of him:

> This Dante was an honourable and ancient citizen of Florence . . .
> a great scholar in almost every branch of learning, although he was
> a layman: he was a great poet and philosopher, and a perfect
> rhetorician both in prose and verse, and in public debate he was a
> very noble speaker; in rime he was supreme, with the most polished
> and beautiful style that ever had been in our language, up to his
> time and since.

The distinguished Giovanni Boccaccio (1313–1375), author of the *Decameron*, who for his *Vita di Dante* collected impressions of Dante from many of his surviving acquaintances, gave the following description of him:

> Our poet was of middle height, and after he had reached mature years he walked with somewhat of a stoop; his gait was grave and sedate; and he was ever clothed in most seemly garments, his dress being suited to the ripeness of his years. His face was long, his nose aquiline, his eyes rather large than small, his jaws heavy, with the under lip projecting beyond the upper. His complexion was dark, and his hair and beard thick, black, and crisp; and his countenance always sad and thoughtful. Whence it happened one day in Verona (the fame of his writings having by that time been spread abroad everywhere, and especially of that part of his *Commedia* to which he gave the title of Hell, and he himself being known by sight to many men and women), that as he passed before a doorway where several women were sitting, one of them said to the others in a low voice, but not so low but that she was plainly heard by him and by those with him, 'Do you see the man who goes down to Hell, and returns at his pleasure, and brings back news of those who are below?' To which one of the others answered in all simplicity: 'Indeed, what you say must be true; don't you see how his beard is crisped and his colour darkened by the heat and smoke down below?' Dante, hearing those words behind him, and perceiving that they were spoken by the women in perfect good faith, was not ill pleased that they should have such an opinion of him, and smiling a little passed on his way.

Dante's first work, *La Vita Nuova*, was written c. 1293 when the poet was probably in his late twenties, and it is many things to many scholars: a book of collected lyrics written in the poet's youth, a treatise for poets on the art of poetry, an autobiography in verse, as well as an introduction to *The Divine Comedy*. The book alternates between poetry and the prose that expounds it, with the character of Beatrice (whose name means "she who confers blessings") as its centerpiece and inspiration. Dante and Beatrice Portinari first met when the two were both about nine years old. They were each betrothed to others, so their love was never consummated; and Beatrice died in 1290 at the age of twenty-five. Yet from these few facts sprung one of the great love stories of all time and the first of modern literature. *La Vita Nuova* is usually translated to mean "The New Life," and is generally interpreted as referring to Dante's life made new by his love for Beatrice. To cite Boccaccio, again:

> [Dante], first of all, while his tears for the death of Beatrice were yet fresh, when he was nigh upon his 26th year, collected together in a

little volume, to which he gave the title *La Vita Nuova*, certain small works, such as sonnets and canzoni, composed by him in rime at divers times before, and of marvellous beauty. Above each of these, severally and in order, he wrote the occasions which had moved him to compose them; and below he added the divisions of each poem.

Dante broke new ground with this work especially with respect to the prose commentaries, i.e., "the occasions which had moved him to compose [the poems]." For one thing, he wrote these in the vernacular Italian instead of the traditional Latin; and more importantly, Dante chose to admit reality into the strict and exclusionary realm of poetic convention by telling the reader about the events—external, as well as emotional and imaginative—that inspired the poems.

A brief word on the translator: Dante Gabriel Rossetti (1828–1882), English poet and painter, was born in London to a remarkable family who had strong cultural ties to both England and Italy. His father was an exiled Italian patriot and man of letters who had a great reverence for Italian poetry, particularly Dante Alighieri's *La Vita Nuova* and *The Divine Comedy*, a reverence he passed along to his children. After completing his general education, his charismatic son Dante Gabriel Rossetti vacillated between poetry and painting as a vocation. Among many other notable accomplishments, he was the founder of the Pre-Raphaelite Brotherhood with six other members—nearly all students of the Royal Academy—who advocated a reform of the arts in England, and whose efforts did indeed achieve some lasting influence throughout Europe and America. The art critic John Ruskin—who was also one of Rossetti's patrons—described him as "a great Italian lost in the Inferno of London." One of Rossetti's most important works is *The Early Italian Poets from Ciullo d'Alcamo to Dante Alighieri (1100–1200–1300): in the original metres, together with Dante's Vita Nuova* (1861), a collection of translations of the so-called *stil novist* (or "new style") poetry; this volume had a considerable impact on the English poets who followed.

LA VITA NUOVA

(The New Life)

I

IN THAT part of the book of my memory before the which is little that can be read, there is a rubric, saying, "Here beginneth the New Life." Under such rubric I find written many things; and among them the words which I purpose to copy into this little book; if not all of them, at the least their substance.

II

Nine times already since my birth had the heaven of light returned to the selfsame point almost, as concerns its own revolution, when first the glorious Lady of my mind was made manifest to mine eyes; even she who was called Beatrice by many who knew not wherefore. She had already been in this life for so long as that, within her time, the starry heaven had moved towards the Eastern quarter one of the twelve parts of a degree: so that she appeared to me at the beginning of her ninth year almost, and I saw her almost at the end of my ninth year. Her dress, on that day, was of a most noble colour, a subdued and goodly crimson, girdled and adorned in such sort as best suited with her very tender age. At that moment, I say most truly that the spirit of life, which hath its dwelling in the secretest chamber of the heart, began to tremble so violently that the least pulses of my body shook therewith; and in trembling it said these words: "Here is a deity stronger than I; who, coming, shall rule over me." At that moment the animate spirit, which dwelleth in the lofty chamber whither all the senses carry their perceptions, was filled with wonder, and speaking more especially unto the spirits of the eyes, said these words: "Your beatitude hath now been made manifest unto you." At that moment the natural spirit, which dwelleth there were our nourishment is administered, began to weep, and in weeping said these words: "Alas! how often shall I be disturbed from this time forth." I say that, from that time forward, Love quite governed my soul; which was immediately espoused to him, and with so

1

safe and undisputed a lordship, (by virtue of strong imagination) that I had nothing left for it but to do all his bidding continually. He often-times commanded me to seek if I might see this youngest of the Angels: wherefore I in my boyhood often went in search of her, and found her so noble and praiseworthy that certainly of her might have been said those words of the poet Homer, "She seemed not to be the daughter of a mortal man, but of God." And albeit her image, that was with me al-ways, was an exultation of Love to subdue me, it was yet of so perfect a quality that it never allowed me to be overruled by Love without the faithful counsel of reason, whensoever such counsel was useful to be heard. But seeing that were I to dwell overmuch on the passions and doings of such early youth, my words might be counted something fab-ulous, I will therefore put them aside; and passing many things that may be conceived by the pattern of these, I will come to such as are writ in my memory with a better distinctness.

III

After the lapse of so many days that nine years exactly were com-pleted since the above-written appearance of this most gracious being, on the last of those days it happened that the same wonderful lady ap-peared to me dressed all in pure white, between two gentle ladies elder than she. And passing through a street, she turned her eyes thither where I stood sorely abashed: and by her unspeakable courtesy, which is now guerdoned* in the Great Cycle, she saluted me with so virtuous a bearing that I seemed then and there to behold the very limits of blessedness. The hour of her most sweet salutation was certainly the ninth of that day; and because it was the first time that any words from her reached mine ears, I came into such sweetness that I parted thence as one intoxicated. And betaking me to the loneliness of mine own room, I fell to thinking of this most courteous lady, thinking of whom I was overtaken by a pleasant slumber, wherein a marvellous vision was presented to me: for there appeared to be in my room a mist of the colour of fire, within the which I discerned the figure of a lord of terri-ble aspect to such as should gaze upon him, but who seemed there-withal to rejoice inwardly that it was a marvel to see. Speaking he said many things, among the which I could understand but few; and of these, this: "I am thy master." In his arms it seemed to me that a person was sleeping, covered only with a blood-coloured cloth; upon whom looking very attentively, I knew that it was the lady of the salutation who had deigned the day before to salute me. And he who held her held also in his hand a thing that was burning in flames; and he said to

---

*"guerdon": reward, recompense (ed.)

me, "Behold thy heart." But when he had remained with me a little while, I thought that he set himself to awaken her that slept; after the which he made her to eat that thing which flamed in his hand; and she ate as one fearing. Then, having waited again a space, all his joy was turned into most bitter weeping; and as he wept he gathered the lady into his arms, and it seemed to me that he went with her up towards heaven: whereby such a great anguish came upon me that my light slumber could not endure through it, but was suddenly broken. And immediately having considered, I knew that the hour wherein this vision had been made manifest to me was the fourth hour (which is to say, the first of the nine last hours) of the night. Then, musing on what I had seen, I proposed to relate the same to many poets who were famous in that day: and for that I had myself in some sort the art of discoursing with rhyme, I resolved on making a sonnet, in the which, having saluted all such as are subject unto Love, and entreated them to expound my vision, I should write unto them those things which I had seen in my sleep. And the sonnet I made was this:

> To every heart which the sweet pain doth move,
>   And unto which these words may now be brought
>   For true interpretation and kind thought,
>   Be greeting in our Lord's name, which is Love.
> Of those long hours wherein the stars, above,
>   Wake and keep watch, the [fourth]* was almost nought
>   When Love was shown me with such terrors fraught
>   As may not carelessly be spoken of.
> He seem'd like one who is full of joy, and had
>   My heart within his hand, and on his arm
>   My lady, with a mantle round her, slept;
> Whom (having waken'd her) anon he made
>   To eat that heart; she ate, as fearing harm.
>   Then he went out; and as he went, he wept.

This sonnet is divided into two parts. In the first part I give greeting, and ask an answer; in the second, I signify what thing has to be answered to. The second part commences here, "Of those long hours."

To this sonnet I received many answers, conveying many different opinions; of the which, one was sent by him whom I now call the first among my friends; and it began thus, "Unto my thinking thou beheld'st all worth." And indeed, it was when he learned that I was he who had sent those rhymes to him, that our friendship commenced. But the true

---

*Scholars have noted that Rossetti incorrectly translated this reference as the "third." (ed.)

meaning of that vision was not then perceived by any one, though it be now evident to the least skilful.

IV

From that night forth, the natural functions of my body began to be vexed and impeded, for I was given up wholly to thinking of this most gracious creature: whereby in short space I became so weak and so reduced that it was irksome to many of my friends to look upon me; while others, being moved by spite, went about to discover what it was my wish should be concealed. Wherefore I, (perceiving the drift of their unkindly questions,) by Love's will, who directed me according to the counsels of reason, told them how it was Love himself who had thus dealt with me: and I said so, because the thing was so plainly to be discerned in my countenance that there was no longer any means of concealing it. But when they went on to ask, "And by whose help hath Love done this?" I looked in their faces smiling, and spake no word in return.

V

Now it fell on a day, that this most gracious creature was sitting where words were to be heard of the Queen of Glory; and I was in a place whence mine eyes could behold their beatitude: and betwixt her and me, in a direct line, there sat another lady of a pleasant favour; who looked round at me many times, marvelling at my continued gaze which seemed to have *her* for its object. And many perceived that she thus looked: so that departing thence, I heard it whispered after me, "Look you to what a pass *such a lady* hath brought him"; and in saying this they named her who had been midway between the most gentle Beatrice, and mine eyes. Therefore I was reassured, and knew that for that day my secret had not become manifest. Then immediately it came into my mind that I might make use of this lady as a screen to the truth: and so well did I play my part that the most of those who had hitherto watched and wondered at me, now imagined they had found me out. By her means I kept my secret concealed till some years were gone over; and for my better security, I even made divers rhymes in her honour; whereof I shall here write only as much as concerneth the most gentle Beatrice, which is but a very little.

VI

Moreover, about the same time while this lady was a screen for so much love on my part, I took the resolution to set down the name of this most gracious creature accompanied with many other women's names, and especially with hers whom I spake of. And to this end I put together the names of sixty the most beautiful ladies in that city where God had placed mine own lady; and these names I introduced in an epistle in the form of a *sirvent,** which it is not my intention to transcribe here. Neither should I have said anything of this matter, did I not wish to take note of a certain strange thing, to wit: that having written the list, I found my lady's name would not stand otherwise than ninth in order among the names of these ladies.

VII

Now it so chanced with her by whose means I had thus long time concealed my desire, that it behoved her to leave the city I speak of, and to journey afar: wherefore I, being sorely perplexed at the loss of so excellent a defence, had more trouble than even I could before have supposed. And thinking that if I spoke not somewhat mournfully of her departure, my former counterfeiting would be the more quickly perceived, I determined that I would make a grievous sonnet thereof; the which I will write here, because it hath certain words in it whereof my lady was the immediate cause, as will be plain to him that understands. And the sonnet was this:

> All ye that pass along Love's trodden way,
>   Pause ye awhile and say
>   If there be any grief like unto mine:
> I pray you that you hearken a short space
>   Patiently, if my case
>   Be not a piteous marvel and a sign.
>
> Love (never, certes,† for my worthless part,
>   But of his own great heart,)
>   Vouchsafed to me a life so calm and sweet
> That oft I heard folk question as I went
>   What such great gladness meant:—
>   They spoke of it behind me in the street.
>
> But now that fearless bearing is all gone
>   Which with Love's hoarded wealth was given me;
>   Till I am grown to be
> So poor that I have dread to think thereon.

---

*"*sirvent*": a moral poem or song—usually satiric—performed by troubadours of the Middle Ages. (ed.)
†"certes": certainly (ed.)

> And thus it is that I, being like as one
>   Who is ashamed and hides his poverty,
>   Without seem full of glee,
>   And let my heart within travail and moan.

This poem has two principal parts; for, in the first, I mean to call the Faithful of Love in those words of Jeremias the Prophet, "Is it nothing to you, all ye that pass by? behold, and see if there be any sorrow like unto my sorrow," and to pray them to stay and hear me. In the second, I tell where Love had placed me, with a meaning other than that which the last part of the poem shows, and I say what I have lost. The second part begins here: "Love (never, certes)."

VIII

A certain while after the departure of that lady, it pleased the Master of the Angels to call into His glory a damsel, young and of a gentle presence, who had been very lovely in the city I speak of: and I saw her body lying without its soul among many ladies, who held a pitiful weeping. Whereupon, remembering that I had seen her in the company of excellent Beatrice, I could not hinder myself from a few tears; and weeping, I conceived to say somewhat of her death, in guerdon of having seen her somewhile with my lady; which thing I spake of in the latter end of the verses that I writ in this matter, as he will discern who understands. And I wrote two sonnets, which are these:

> Weep, Lovers, sith Love's very self doth weep,
>   And sith the cause for weeping is so great;
>   When now so many dames, of such estate
>   In worth, show with their eyes a grief so deep:
> For Death the churl has laid his leaden sleep
>   Upon a damsel who was fair of late,
>   Defacing all our earth should celebrate, —
>   Yea all save virtue, which the soul doth keep.
> Now hearken how much Love did honour her.
>   I myself saw him in his proper form
>   Bending above the motionless sweet dead,
>   And often gazing into Heaven; for there
>   The soul now sits which when her life was warm
>   Dwelt with the joyful beauty that is fled.

This first sonnet is divided into three parts. In the first, I call and beseech the Faithful of Love to weep; and I say that their Lord weeps, and that they, hearing the reason why he weeps, shall be more minded to listen to me. In the second, I relate this reason. In the third, I speak of honour done by Love to this Lady. The second part begins here, "When now so many dames"; the third here, "Now hearken."

> Death, always cruel, Pity's foe in chief,
> Mother who brought forth grief,
> Merciless judgement and without appeal!
> Since thou alone hast made my heart to feel
> This sadness and unweal,*
> My tongue upbraideth thee without relief.
>
> And now (for I must rid thy name of ruth)
> Behoves me speak the truth
> Touching thy cruelty and wickedness:
> Not that they be not known; but ne'ertheless
> I would give hate more stress
> With them that feed on love in very sooth.
>
> Out of this world thou hast driven courtesy,
> And virtue, dearly prized in womanhood;
> And out of youth's gay mood
> The lovely lightness is quite gone through thee.
>
> Whom now I mourn, no man shall learn from me
> Save by the measure of these praises given.
> Whoso deserves not Heaven
> May never hope to have her company.

This poem is divided into four parts. In the first I address Death by certain proper names of hers. In the second, speaking to her, I tell the reason why I am moved to denounce her. In the third, I rail against her. In the fourth, I turn to speak to a person undefined, although defined in my own conception. The second part commences here, "Since thou alone"; the third here, "And now (for I must)"; the fourth here, "Whoso deserves not."

IX

Some days after the death of this lady, I had occasion to leave the city I speak of, and to go thitherwards where she abode who had formerly been my protection; albeit the end of my journey reached not altogether so far. And notwithstanding that I was visibly in the company of many, the journey was so irksome that I had scarcely sighing enough to ease my heart's heaviness; seeing that as I went, I left my beatitude behind me. Wherefore it came to pass that he who ruled me by virtue of

---

*"unweal": unhappiness (ed.)

my most gentle lady was made visible to my mind, in the light habit of
a traveller, coarsely fashioned. He appeared to me troubled, and looked
always on the ground; saving only that sometimes his eyes were turned
towards a river which was clear and rapid, and which flowed along the
path I was taking. And then I thought that Love called me and said to
me these words: "I come from that lady who was so long thy surety; for
the matter of whose return, I know that it may not be. Wherefore I have
taken that heart which I made thee leave with her, and do bear it unto
another lady, who, as she was, shall be thy surety"; (and when he
named her, I knew her well). "And of these words I have spoken, if
thou shouldst speak any again, let it be in such sort as that none shall
perceive thereby that thy love was feigned for her, which thou must
now feign for another." And when he had spoken thus, all my imagin-
ing was gone suddenly, for it seemed to me that Love became a part of
myself: so that, changed as it were in mine aspect, I rode on full of
thought the whole of that day, and with heavy sighing. And the day
being over, I wrote this sonnet:

> A day agone, as I rode sullenly
>   Upon a certain path that liked me not,
>   I met Love midway while the air was hot,
>   Clothed lightly as a wayfarer might be.
> And for the cheer he show'd, he seem'd to me
>   As one who hath lost lordship he had got;
>   Advancing tow'rds me full of sorrowful thought,
>   Bowing his forehead so that none should see.
> Then as I went, he call'd me by my name,
>   Saying: "I journey since the morn was dim
>   Thence where I made thy heart to be: which now
> I needs must bear unto another dame."
>   Wherewith so much pass'd into me of him
>   That he was gone, and I discern'd not how.

*This sonnet has three parts. In the first part, I tell how I met Love and
of his aspect. In the second, I tell what he said to me, although not in
full, through the fear I had of discovering my secret. In the third, I say
how he disappeared. The second part commences here, "Then as I went";
the third here, "Wherewith so much."*

X

On my return, I set myself to seek out that lady whom my master had
named to me while I journeyed sighing. And because I would be brief,
I will now narrate that in a short while I made her my surety, in such
sort that the matter was spoken of by many in terms scarcely courteous;

through the which I had oftenwhiles many troublesome hours. And by this it happened (to wit: by this false and evil rumour which seemed to misfame me of vice), that she who was the destroyer of all evil and the queen of all good, coming where I was, denied me her most sweet salutation, in the which alone was my blessedness. And here it is fitting for me to depart a little from this present matter, that it may be rightly understood of what surpassing virtue her salutation was to me.

XI

To the which end I say that when she appeared in any place, it seemed to me, by the hope of her excellent salutation, that there was no man mine enemy any longer; and such warmth of charity came upon me that most certainly in that moment I would have pardoned whosoever had done me an injury; and if one should then have questioned me concerning any matter, I could only have said unto him "Love," with a countenance clothed in humbleness. And what time she made ready to salute me, the spirit of Love, destroying all other perceptions, thrust forth the feeble spirits of mine eyes, saying, "Do homage unto your mistress," and putting itself in their place to obey: so that he who would, might then have beheld Love, beholding the lids of mine eyes shake. And when this most gentle lady gave her salutation, Love, so far from being a medium beclouding mine intolerable beatitude, then bred in me such an overpowering sweetness that my body, being all subjected thereto, remained many times helpless and passive. Whereby it is made manifest that in her salutation alone was there any beatitude for me, which then very often went beyond my endurance.

XII

And now, resuming my discourse, I will go on to relate that when, for the first time, this beatitude was denied me, I became possessed with such grief that parting myself from others, I went into a lonely place to bathe the ground with most bitter tears: and when, by this heat of weeping, I was somewhat relieved, I betook myself to my chamber, where I could lament unheard. And there, having prayed to the Lady of all Mercies, and having said also, "O Love, aid thou thy servant," I went suddenly asleep like a beaten sobbing child. And in my sleep, towards the middle of it, I seemed to see in the room, seated at my side, a youth in very white raiment, who kept his eyes fixed on me in deep thought. And when he had gazed some time, I thought that he sighed and called to me in these words: "My son, it is time for us to lay aside our counterfeiting." And thereupon I seemed to know him; for the voice was the same wherewith he had spoken at other times in my sleep. Then looking at him, I perceived that he was weeping piteously, and that he seemed to be waiting for me to speak. Wherefore, taking heart, I began thus: "Why weepest thou, Master of all honour?" And he made answer to me: "I am as the centre of a circle, to the which all parts of the circumference bear an equal relation; but with thee it is not thus." And thinking upon his words, they seemed to me obscure; so that again compelling myself unto speech, I asked of him: "What thing is this, Master, that thou hast spoken thus darkly?" To the which he made answer in the vulgar tongue: "Demand no more than may be useful to thee." Whereupon I began to discourse with him concerning her salutation which she had denied me; and when I had questioned him of the cause, he said these words: "Our Beatrice hath heard from certain persons, that the lady whom I named to thee while thou journeyedst full of sighs, is sorely disquieted by thy solicitations: and therefore this most gracious creature, who is the enemy of all disquiet, being fearful of such disquiet, refused to salute thee. For the whole reason (albeit, in very sooth, thy secret must needs have become known to her by familiar observation) it is my will that thou compose certain things in rhyme, in the which thou shalt set forth how strong a mastership I have obtained over thee, through her; and how thou wast hers even from thy childhood. Also do thou call upon him that knoweth these things to bear witness to them, bidding him to speak with her thereof; the which I, who am he, will do willingly. And thus she shall be made to know thy desire; knowing which, she shall know likewise that they were deceived who spake of thee to her. And so write these things, that they shall seem rather to be spoken by a third person; and not directly by thee to her, which is scarce fitting. After the which, send them, not without me, where she may have a chance to hear them; but have them fitted with a pleasant music, into the which I will pass whensoever it needeth." With this speech he was away, and my sleep was broken up. Whereupon, remembering me, I knew that I had beheld this vision during the ninth hour of the day; and I resolved that I would make a ditty, before I left my chamber, according to the words my master had spoken. And this is the ditty that I made:

> Song, 'tis my will that thou do seek out Love,
> And go with him where my dear lady is;
> That so my cause, the which thy harmonies
> Do plead, his better speech may clearly prove.
>
> Thou goest, my Song, in such a courteous kind,
> That even companionless
> Thou may'st rely on thyself anywhere.
> And yet, an thou wouldst get thee a safe mind,
> First unto Love address

Thy steps; whose aid, mayhap, 'twere ill to spare:
Seeing that she to whom thou mak'st thy prayer
Is, as I think, ill-minded unto me,
And that if Love do not companion thee,
Thou'lt have perchance small cheer to tell me of.

With a sweet accent, when thou com'st to her
  Begin thou in these words,
  First having craved a gracious audience:
  "He who hath sent me as his messenger,
  Lady, thus much records,
  An thou but suffer him, in his defence.
  Love, who comes with me, by thine influence
  Can make this man do as it liketh him:
  Wherefore, if this fault *is* or doth but *seem*
  Do thou conceive: for his heart cannot move."

Say to her also: "Lady, his poor heart
  Is so confirm'd in faith
  That all its thoughts are but of serving thee:
  'Twas early thine, and could not swerve apart."
  Then, if she wavereth,
  Bid her ask Love, who knows if these things be.
  And in the end, beg of her modestly
  To pardon so much boldness: saying too: —
  "If thou declare his death to be thy due,
  The thing shall come to pass, as doth behove."

Then pray thou of the Master of all ruth,
  Before thou leave her there,
  That he befriend my cause and plead it well.
  "In guerdon of my sweet rhymes and my truth"
  (Entreat him) "stay with her;
  Let not the hope of thy poor servant fail;
  And if with her thy pleading should prevail,
  Let her look on him and give peace to him."
  Gentle my Song, if good to thee it seem,
  Do this: so worship shall be thine and love.

This ditty is divided into three parts. In the first, I tell it whither to go, and I encourage it, that it may go the more confidently, and I tell it whose company to join if it would go with confidence and without any danger. In the second, I say that which it behoves the ditty to set forth. In the third, I give it leave to start when it pleases, recommending its course to the arms of Fortune. The second part begins here, "With a sweet accent"; the third here, "Gentle my Song." Some might contradict me, and say that they understand not whom I address in the second person, seeing that the ditty is merely the very words I am speaking. And therefore I say that this doubt I intend to solve and clear up in this little book itself, at a more difficult passage, and then let him understand who now doubts, or would now contradict as aforesaid.

XIII

After this vision I have recorded, and having written those words which Love had dictated to me, I began to be harassed with many and divers thoughts, by each of which I was sorely tempted; and in especial, there were four among them that left me no rest. The first was this: "Certainly the lordship of Love is good; seeing that it diverts the mind from all mean things." The second was this: "Certainly the lordship of Love is evil; seeing that the more homage his servants pay to him, the more grievous and painful are the torments wherewith he torments them." The third was this: "The name of Love is so sweet in the hearing that it would not seem possible for its effects to be other than sweet; seeing that the name must needs be like unto the thing named: as it is written: 'Names are the consequents of things.'" And the fourth was this: "The lady whom Love hath chosen out to govern thee is not as other ladies, whose hearts are easily moved." And by each one of these thoughts I was so sorely assailed that I was like unto him who doubteth which path to take, and wishing to go, goeth not. And if I bethought myself to seek out some point at the which all these paths might be found to meet, I discerned but one way, and that irked me; to wit, to call upon Pity, and to commend myself unto her. And it was then that, feeling a desire to write somewhat thereof in rhyme, I wrote this sonnet:

> All my thoughts always speak to me of Love,
>> Yet have between themselves such difference
>> That while one bids me bow with mind and sense,
>> A second saith, "Go to: look thou above";
> The third one, hoping, yields me joy enough;
>> And with the last come tears, I scarce know whence:
>> All of them craving pity in sore suspense,
>> Trembling with fears that the heart knoweth of.
> And thus, being all unsure which path to take,
>> Wishing to speak I know not what to say,
>> And lose myself in amorous wanderings:
> Until, (my peace with all of them to make,)
>> Unto mine enemy I needs must pray,
>> My lady Pity, for the help she brings.

This sonnet may be divided into four parts. In the first, I say and propound that all my thoughts are concerning Love. In the second, I say that they are diverse, and I relate their diversity. In the third, I say wherein they all seem to agree. In the fourth, I say that, wishing to speak of Love, I know not from which of these thoughts to take my argument; and that if I would take it from all, I shall have to call upon mine enemy, my lady Pity. "Lady" I say as in a scornful mode of speech. The second begins here, "Yet have between themselves"; the third, "All of them craving"; the fourth, "And thus."

XIV

After this battling with many thoughts, it chanced on a day that my most gracious lady was with a gathering of ladies in a certain place; to the which I was conducted by a friend of mine; he thinking to do me a great pleasure by showing me the beauty of so many women. Then I, hardly knowing whereunto he conducted me, but trusting in him (who yet was leading his friend to the last verge of life), made question: "To what end are we come among these ladies?" and he answered: "To the end that they may be worthily served." And they were assembled around a gentlewoman who was given in marriage on that day; the custom of the city being that these should bear her company when she sat down for the first time at table in the house of her husband. Therefore I, as was my friend's pleasure, resolved to stay with him and do honour to those ladies. But as soon as I had thus resolved, I began to feel a faintness and a throbbing at my left side, which soon took possession of my whole body. Whereupon I remember that I covertly leaned my back unto a painting that ran round the walls of that house; and being fearful lest my trembling should be discerned of them, I lifted mine eyes to look on those ladies, and then first perceived among them the excellent Beatrice. And when I perceived her, all my senses were overpowered by the great lordship that Love obtained, finding himself so near unto that most gracious being, until nothing but the spirits of sight remained to me; and even these remained driven out of their own instruments because Love entered into that honoured place of theirs, that so he might the better behold her. And although I was other than at first, I grieved for the spirits so expelled which kept up a sore lament, saying: "If he had not in this wise thrust us forth, we also should behold the marvel of this lady." By this, many of her friends, having discerned my confusion, began to wonder; and together with herself, kept whispering of me and mocking me. Whereupon my friend, who knew not what to conceive, took me by the hands, and drawing me forth from among them, required to know what ailed me. Then, having first held me at quiet for a space until my perceptions were come back to me, I made answer to my friend: "Of a surety I have now set my feet on that point of life, beyond the which he must not pass who would return." Afterwards, leaving him, I went back to the room where I had wept before; and again weeping and ashamed, said: "If this lady but knew of my condition, I do not think that she would thus mock at me; nay, I am sure that she must needs feel some pity." And in my weeping I bethought me to write certain words in the which, speaking to her, I should signify the occasion of my disfigurement, telling her also how I knew that she had no knowledge thereof: which, if it were known, I was certain must move others to pity. And then, because I hoped that peradventure it might come into her hearing, I wrote this sonnet:

> Even as the others mock, thou mockest me;
> > Not dreaming, noble lady, whence it is
> > That I am taken with strange semblances,
> > Seeing thy face which is so fair to see:
> For else, compassion would not suffer thee
> > To grieve my heart with such harsh scoffs as these.
> > Lo! Love, when thou art present, sits at ease,
> > And bears his mastership so mightily,
> That all my troubled senses he thrusts out,
> > Sorely tormenting some, and slaying some,
> > Till none but he is left and has free range
> To gaze on thee. This makes my face to change
> > Into another's; while I stand all dumb,
> > And hear my senses clamour in their rout.

This sonnet I divide not into parts, because a division is only made to open the meaning of the thing divided: and this, as it is sufficiently manifest through the reasons given, has no need of division. True it is that, amid the words whereby is shown the occasion of this sonnet, dubious words are to be found; namely, when I say that Love kills all my spirits, but that the visual remain in life, only outside of their own instruments. And this difficulty it is impossible for any to solve who is not in equal guise liege unto Love; and, to those who are so, that is manifest which would clear up the dubious words. And therefore it were not well for me to expound this difficulty, inasmuch as my speaking would be either fruitless or else superfluous.

XV

A while after this strange disfigurement, I became possessed with a strong conception which left me but very seldom, and then to return quickly. And it was this: "Seeing that thou comest into such scorn by the companionship of this lady, wherefore seekest thou to behold her?

If she should ask thee this thing, what answer couldst thou make unto her? yea, even though thou wert master of all thy faculties, and in no way hindered from answering." Unto the which, another very humble thought said in reply: "If I were master of all my faculties, and in no way hindered from answering, I would tell her that no sooner do I image to myself her marvellous beauty than I am possessed with the desire to behold her, the which is of so great strength that it kills and destroys in my memory all those things which might oppose it; and it is therefore that the great anguish I have endured thereby is yet not enough to restrain me from seeking to behold her." And then, because of these thoughts, I resolved to write somewhat, wherein, having pleaded mine excuse, I should tell her of what I felt in her presence. Whereupon I wrote this sonnet:

> The thoughts are broken in my memory,
>> Thou lovely Joy, whene'er I see thy face;
>> When thou art near me, Love fills up the space,
>> Often repeating, "If death irk thee, fly."
> My face shows my heart's colour, verily,
>> Which, fainting, seeks for any leaning-place
>> Till, in the drunken terror of disgrace,
>> The very stones seem to be shrieking, "Die!"
> It were a grievous sin, if one should not
>> Strive then to comfort my bewilder'd mind
>> (Though merely with a simple pitying)
> For the great anguish which thy scorn has wrought
>> In the dead sight o' the eyes grown nearly blind,
>> Which look for death as for a blessed thing.

This sonnet is divided into two parts. In the first, I tell the cause why I abstain not from coming to this lady. In the second, I tell what befalls me through coming to her; and this part begins here, "When thou art near." And also this second part divides into five distinct statements. For, in the first, I say what Love, counselled by Reason, tells me when I am near the lady. In the second, I set forth the state of my heart by the example of the face. In the third, I say how all ground of trust fails me. In the fourth, I say that he sins who shows not pity of me, which would give me some comfort. In the last, I say why people should take pity; namely, for the piteous look which comes into mine eyes; which piteous look is destroyed, that is, appeareth not unto others, through the jeering of this lady, who draws to the like action those who peradventure would see this piteousness. The second part begins here, "My face shows"; the third, "Till, in the drunken terror"; the fourth, "It were a grievous sin"; the fifth, "For the great anguish."

XVI

Thereafter, this sonnet bred in me desire to write down in verse four other things touching my condition, the which things it seemed to me that I had not yet made manifest. The first among these was the grief that possessed me very often, remembering the strangeness which Love wrought in me; the second was, how Love many times assailed me so suddenly and with such strength that I had no other life remaining except a thought which spake of my lady; the third was, how when Love did battle with me in this wise, I would rise up all colourless, if so I might see my lady, conceiving that the sight of her would defend me against the assault of Love, and altogether forgetting that which her presence brought unto me; and the fourth was, how when I saw her, the sight not only defended me not, but took away the little life that remained to me. And I said these four things in a sonnet, which is this:

> At whiles (yea oftentimes) I muse over
>   The quality of anguish that is mine
>   Through Love: then pity makes my voice to pine
>   Saying, "Is any else thus, anywhere?"
> Love smiteth me, whose strength is ill to bear;
>   So that of all my life is left no sign
>   Except one thought; and that, because 'tis thine
>   Leaves not the body but abideth there.
> And then if I, whom other aid forsook,
>   Would aid myself, and innocent of art
>   Would fain have sight of thee as a last hope,
> No sooner do I lift mine eyes to look
>   Than the blood seems as shaken from my heart,
>   And all my pulses beat at once and stop.

This sonnet is divided into four parts, four things being therein narrated; and as these are set forth above, I only proceed to distinguish the parts by their beginnings. Wherefore I say that the second part begins, "Love smiteth me"; the third, "And then if I"; the fourth, "No sooner do I lift."

XVII

After I had written these last three sonnets, wherein I spake unto my lady, telling her almost the whole of my condition, it seemed to me that I should be silent, having said enough concerning myself. But albeit I spake not to her again, yet it behoved me afterward to write of another matter, more noble than the foregoing. And for that the occasion of what I then wrote may be found pleasant in the hearing, I will relate it as briefly as I may.

XVIII

Through the sore change in mine aspect, the secret of my heart was now understood of many. Which thing being thus, there came a day when certain ladies to whom it was well known (they having been with me at divers times in my trouble) were met together for the pleasure of gentle company. And as I was going that way by chance, (but I think rather by the will of fortune,) I heard one of them call unto me, and she that called was a lady of very sweet speech. And when I had come close up with them, and perceived that they had not among them mine excellent lady, I was reassured; and saluted them, asking of their pleasure. The ladies were many; divers of whom were laughing one to another, while divers gazed at me as though I should speak anon. But when I still spake not, one of them, who before had been talking with another, addressed me by my name, saying, "To what end lovest thou this lady, seeing that thou canst not support her presence? Now tell us this thing, that we may know it: for certainly the end of such a love must be worthy of knowledge." And when she had spoken these words, not she only, but all they that were with her, began to observe me, waiting for my reply. Whereupon, I said thus unto them: "Ladies, the end and aim of my love was but the salutation of that lady of whom I conceive that ye are speaking; wherein alone I found that beatitude which is the goal of desire. And now that it hath pleased her to deny me this, Love, my Master, of his great goodness, hath placed all my beatitude there where my hope will not fail me." Then those ladies began to talk closely together; and as I have seen snow fall among the rain, so was their talk mingled with sighs. But after a little, that lady who had been the first to address me, addressed me again in these words: "We pray thee that thou wilt tell us wherein abideth this thy beatitude." And answering, I said but thus much: "In those words that do praise my lady." To the which she rejoined, "If thy speech were true, those words that thou didst write concerning thy condition would have been written with another intent." Then I, being almost put to shame because of her answer, went out from among them; and as I walked, I said within myself: "Seeing that there is so much beatitude in those words which do praise my lady, wherefore hath my speech of her been different?" And then I resolved that thenceforward I would choose for the theme of my writings only the praise of this most gracious being. But when I had thought exceedingly, it seemed to me that I had taken to myself a theme which was much too lofty, so that I dared not begin; and I remained during several days in the desire of speaking, and the fear of beginning.

XIX

After which it happened, as I passed one day along a path which lay beside a stream of very clear water, that there came upon me a great desire to say somewhat in rhyme; but when I began thinking how I should say it, methought that to speak of her were unseemly, unless I spoke to other ladies in the second person; which is to say, not to *any* other ladies, but only to such as are so called because they are gentle, let alone for mere womanhood. Whereupon I declare that my tongue spake as though by its own impulse, and said, "Ladies that have intelligence in love." These words I laid up in my mind with great gladness, conceiving to take them as my commencement. Wherefore, having returned to the city I spake of, and considered thereof during certain days, I began a poem with this beginning, constructed in the mode which will be seen below in its division. The poem begins here:

Ladies that have intelligence in love,
    Of mine own lady I would speak with you;
    Not that I hope to count her praises through,
    But telling what I may, to ease my mind.
    And I declare that when I speak thereof
    Love sheds such perfect sweetness over me
    That if my courage fail'd not, certainly
    To him my listeners must be all resign'd.
    Wherefore I will not speak in such large kind
    That mine own speech should foil me, which were base;
    But only will discourse of her high grace
    In these poor words, the best that I can find,
    With you alone, dear dames and damozels:
    'Twere ill to speak thereof with any else.

An Angel, of his blessed knowledge, saith
    To God: "Lord, in the world that Thou hast made,
    A miracle in action is display'd
    By reason of a soul whose splendors fare
    Even hither: and since Heaven requireth
    Nought saving her, for her it prayeth Thee,
    Thy Saints crying aloud continually."
    Yet Pity still defends our earthly share
    In that sweet soul; God answering thus the prayer:
    "My well-belovèd, suffer that in peace
    Your hope remain, while so My pleasure is,
    There where one dwells who dreads the loss of her;

And who in Hell unto the doom'd shall say,
'I have look'd on that for which God's chosen pray.'"

My lady is desired in the high Heaven:
  Wherefore, it now behoveth me to tell,
  Saying: Let any maid that would be well
  Esteem'd keep with her: for as she goes by,
  Into foul hearts a deathly chill is driven
  By Love, that makes ill thought to perish there;
  While any who endures to gaze on her
  Must either be made noble, or else die.
  When one deserving to be raised so high
  Is found, 'tis then her power attains its proof,
  Making his heart strong for his soul's behoof
  With the full strength of meek humility.
  Also this virtue owns she, by God's will:
  Who speaks with her can never come to ill.

Love saith concerning her: "How chanceth it
  That flesh, which is of dust, should be thus pure?"
  Then, gazing always, he makes oath: "Forsure,
  This is a creature of God till now unknown."
  She hath that paleness of the pearl that's fit
  In a fair woman, so much and not more;
  She is as high as Nature's skill can soar;
  Beauty is tried by her comparison.
  Whatever her sweet eyes are turn'd upon,
  Spirits of love do issue thence in flame,
  Which through their eyes who then may look on them
  Pierce to the heart's deep chamber every one.
  And in her smile Love's image you may see;
  Whence none can gaze upon her steadfastly.

Dear Song, I know thou wilt hold gentle speech
  With many ladies, when I send thee forth:
  Wherefore, (being mindful that thou hadst thy birth
  From Love, and art a modest, simple child,)
  Whomso thou meetest, say thou this to each:
  "Give me good speed! To her I wend along
  In whose much strength my weakness is made strong."
  And if, i' the end, thou wouldst not be beguiled
  Of all thy labour, seek not the defiled
  And common sort; but rather choose to be
  Where man and woman dwell in courtesy.

> So to the road thou shalt be reconciled,
> And find the lady, and with the lady, Love.
> Commend thou me to each, as doth behove.

This poem, that it may be better understood, I will divide more subtly than the others preceding; and therefore I will make three parts of it. The first part is a proem to the words following. The second is the matter treated of. The third is, as it were, a handmaid to the preceding words. The second begins here, "An Angel"; the third here, "Dear Song, I know." The first part is divided into four. In the first, I say to whom I mean to speak of my lady, and wherefore I will so speak. In the second, I say what she appears to myself to be when I reflect upon her excellence, and what I would utter if I lost not courage. In the third, I say what it is I purpose to speak, so as not to be impeded by faintheartedness. In the fourth, repeating to whom I purpose speaking, I tell the reason why I speak to them. The second begins here, "And I declare"; the third here, "Wherefore I will not speak"; the fourth here, "With you alone." Then, when I say "An Angel," I begin treating of this lady: and this part is divided into two. In the first, I tell what is understood of her in heaven. In the second, I tell what is understood of her on earth: here, "My lady is desired." This second part is divided into two; for, in the first, I speak of her as regards the nobleness of her soul, relating some of her virtues proceeding from her soul; in the second, I speak of her as regards the nobleness of her body, narrating some of her beauties: here, "Love saith concerning her." This second part is divided into two; for, in the first, I speak of certain beauties which belong to the whole person; in the second, I speak of certain beauties which belong to a distinct part of the person: here, "Whatever her sweet eyes." This second part is divided into two; for, in the one, I speak of the eyes, which are the beginning of love; in the second, I speak of the mouth, which is the end of love. And, that every vicious thought may be discarded herefrom, let the reader remember that it is above written that the greeting of this lady, which was an act of her mouth, was the goal of my desires, while I could receive it. Then, when I say, "Dear Song, I know," I add a stanza as it were handmaid to the others, wherein I say what I desire from this my poem. And because this last part is easy to understand, I trouble not myself with more divisions. I say, indeed, that the further to open the meaning of this poem, more minute divisions ought to be used; but nevertheless he who is not of wit enough to understand it by these which have been already made is welcome to leave it alone; for certes* I fear I have communicated its sense to too many by these present divisions, if it so happened that many should hear it.

XX

When this song was a little gone abroad, a certain one of my friends, hearing the same, was pleased to question me, that I should tell him what thing love is; it may be, conceiving from the words thus heard a hope of me beyond my desert. Wherefore I, thinking that after such discourse it were well to say somewhat of the nature of Love, and also in accordance with my friend's desire, proposed to myself to write certain words in the which I should treat of this argument. And the sonnet that I then made is this:

Love and the gentle heart are one same thing,
　　Even as the wise man in his ditty saith.
　　Each, of itself, would be such life in death
　　As rational soul bereft of reasoning.
'Tis Nature makes them when she loves: a king
　　Love is, whose palace where he sojourneth
　　Is call'd the Heart; there draws he quiet breath
　　At first, with brief or longer slumbering.
Then beauty seen in virtuous womankind
　　Will make the eyes desire, and through the heart
　　Send the desiring of the eyes again;
Where often it abides so long enshrined
　　That Love at length out of his sleep will start.
　　And women feel the same for worthy men.

This sonnet is divided into two parts. In the first, I speak of him according to his power. In the second, I speak of him according as his power translates itself into act. The second part begins here, "Then beauty seen." The first is divided into two. In the first, I say in what subject this power exists. In the second, I say how this subject and this power are produced together, and how the one regards the other, as form does matter. The second begins here, "'Tis Nature." Afterwards when I say, "Then beauty seen in virtuous womankind," I say how this power translates itself into act; and, first, how it so translates itself in a man, then how it so translates itself in a woman: here, "And women feel."

XXI

Having treated of love in the foregoing, it appeared to me that I should also say something in praise of my lady, wherein it might be set forth how love manifested itself when produced by her; and how not only she could awaken it where it slept, but where it was not she could marvellously create it. To the which end I wrote another sonnet; and it is this:

My lady carries love within her eyes;
   All that she looks on is made pleasanter;
   Upon her path men turn to gaze at her;
   He whom she greeteth feels his heart to rise,
And droops his troubled visage, full of sighs,
   And of his evil heart is then aware:
   Hate loves, and pride becomes a worshipper.
   O women, help to praise her in somewise.
Humbleness, and the hope that hopeth well,
   By speech of hers into the mind are brought,
   And who beholds is blessed oftenwhiles.
The look she hath when she a little smiles
   Cannot be said, nor holden in the thought;
   'Tis such a new and gracious miracle.

This sonnet has three sections. In the first, I say how this lady brings this power into action by those most noble features, her eyes; and, in the third, I say this same as to that most noble feature, her mouth. And between these two sections is a little section, which asks, as it were, help for the previous section and the subsequent; and it begins here, "O women, help." The third begins here, "Humbleness." The first is divided into three; for, in the first, I say how she with power makes noble that which she looks upon; and this is as much as to say that she brings Love, in power, thither where he is not. In the second, I say how she brings Love, in act, into the hearts of all those whom she sees. In the third, I tell what she afterwards, with virtue, operates upon their hearts. The second begins, "Upon her path"; the third, "He whom she greeteth." Then, when I say, "O women, help," I intimate to whom it is my intention to speak, calling on women to help me to honour her. Then, when I say, "Humbleness," I say that same which is said in the first part, regarding two acts of her mouth, one whereof is her most sweet speech, and the other her marvellous smile. Only, I say not of this last how it operates upon the hearts of others, because memory cannot retain this smile, nor its operation.

XXII

Not many days after this, (it being the will of the most High God, who also from Himself put not away death,) the father of wonderful Beatrice, going out of this life, passed certainly into glory. Thereby it happened, as of very sooth it might not be otherwise, that this lady was made full of the bitterness of grief: seeing that such a parting is very grievous unto those friends who are left, and that no other friendship is like to that between a good parent and a good child; and furthermore considering that this lady was good in the supreme degree, and her father (as by many it hath been truly averred) of exceeding goodness. And because it is the usage of that city that men meet with men in such a grief, and women with women, certain ladies of her companionship gathered themselves unto Beatrice, where she kept alone in her weeping: and as they passed in and out, I could hear them speak concerning her, how she wept. At length two of them went by me, who said: "Certainly she grieveth in such sort that one might die for pity, beholding her." Then, feeling the tears upon my face, I put up my hands to hide them: and had it not been that I hoped to hear more concerning her, (seeing that where I sat, her friends passed continually in and out,) I should assuredly have gone thence to be alone, when I felt the tears come. But as I still sat in that place, certain ladies again passed near me, who were saying among themselves: "Which of us shall be joyful any more, who have listened to this lady in her piteous sorrow?" And there were others who said as they went by me: "He that sitteth here could not weep more if he had beheld her as we have beheld her"; and again: "He is so altered that he seemeth not as himself." And still as the ladies passed to and fro, I could hear them speak after this fashion of her and of me. Wherefore afterwards, having considered and perceiving that there was herein matter for poesy, I resolved that I would write certain rhymes in the which should be contained all that those ladies had said. And because I would willingly have spoken to them if it had not been for discreetness, I made in my rhymes as though I had spoken and they had answered me. And therefore I wrote two sonnets; in the first of which I addressed them as I would fain have done; and in the second related their answer, using the speech that I had heard from them, as though it had been spoken unto myself. And the sonnets are these:

> You that thus wear a modest countenance
>> With lids weigh'd down by the heart's heaviness,
>> Whence come you, that among you every face
>> Appears the same, for its pale troubled glance?
> Have you beheld my lady's face, perchance,
>> Bow'd with the grief that Love makes full of grace?
>> Say now, "This thing is thus"; as my heart says,
>> Marking your grave and sorrowful advance.
> And if indeed you come from where she sighs
>> And mourns, may it please you (for his heart's relief)
>> To tell how it fares with her unto him
> Who knows that you have wept, seeing your eyes,
>> And is so grieved with looking on your grief
>> That his heart trembles and his sight grows dim.

This sonnet is divided into two parts. In the first, I call and ask these ladies whether they come from her, telling them that I think they do, because they return the nobler. In the second, I pray them to tell me of her: and the second begins here, "And if indeed."

> Canst thou indeed be he that still would sing
> Of our dear lady unto none but us?
> For though thy voice confirms that it is thus,
> Thy visage might another witness bring.
> And wherefore is thy grief so sore a thing
> That grieving thou mak'st others dolorous?
> Hast thou too seen her weep, that thou from us
> Canst not conceal thine inward sorrowing?
> Nay, leave our woe to us: let us alone:
> 'Twere sin if one should strive to soothe our woe,
> For in her weeping we have heard her speak:
> Also her look's so full of her heart's moan
> That they who should behold her, looking so,
> Must fall aswoon, feeling all life grow weak.

This sonnet has four parts, as the ladies in whose person I reply had four forms of answer. And, because these are sufficiently shown above, I stay not to explain the purport of the parts, and therefore I only discriminate them. The second begins here, "And wherefore is thy grief"; the third here, "Nay, leave our woe"; the fourth, "Also her look."

XXIII

A few days after this, my body became afflicted with a painful infirmity, whereby I suffered bitter anguish for many days, which at last brought me unto such weakness that I could no longer move. And I remember that on the ninth day, being overcome with intolerable pain, a thought came into my mind concerning my lady: but when it had a little nourished this thought, my mind returned to its brooding over mine enfeebled body. And then perceiving how frail a thing life is, even though health keep with it, the matter seemed to me so pitiful that I could not choose but weep; and weeping I said within myself: "Certainly it must some time come to pass that the very gentle Beatrice will die." Then, feeling bewildered, I closed mine eyes; and my brain began to be in travail as the brain of one frantic, and to have such imaginations as here follow. And at the first, it seemed to me that I saw certain faces of women with their hair loosened, which called out to me, "Thou shalt surely die"; after the which, other terrible and unknown appearances said unto me, "Thou art dead." At length, as my phantasy held on in its wanderings, I came to be I knew not where, and to behold a throng of dishevelled ladies wonderfully sad, who kept going

hither and thither weeping. Then the sun went out, so that the stars
showed themselves, and they were of such a colour that I knew they
must be weeping: and it seemed to me that the birds fell dead out of
the sky, and that there were great earthquakes. With that, while I won-
dered in my trance, and was filled with a grievous fear, I conceived that
a certain friend came unto me and said: "Hast thou not heard? She that
was thine excellent lady hath been taken out of life." Then I began to
weep very piteously; and not only in mine imagination, but with mine
eyes, which were wet with tears. And I seemed to look towards Heaven,
and to behold a multitude of angels who were returning upwards, hav-
ing before them an exceedingly white cloud: and these angels were
singing together gloriously, and the words of their song were these:
"Hosanna in the highest": and there was no more that I heard. Then
my heart that was so full of love said unto me: "It is true that our lady
lieth dead": and it seemed to me that I went to look upon the body
wherein that blessed and most noble spirit had had its abiding-place.
And so strong was this idle imagining, that it made me to behold my
lady in death; whose head certain ladies seemed to be covering with a
white veil; and who was so humble of her aspect that it was as though
she had said, "I have attained to look on the beginning of peace." And
therewithal I came unto such humility by the light of her, that I cried
out upon Death, saying: "Now come unto me, and be not bitter against
me any longer: surely, there where thou hast been, thou hast learned
gentleness. Wherefore come now unto me who do greatly desire thee:
seest thou not that I wear thy colour already?" And when I had seen all
those offices performed that are fitting to be done unto the dead, it
seemed to me that I went back unto mine own chamber, and looked
up towards heaven. And so strong was my phantasy, that I wept again
in very truth, and said with my true voice: "O excellent soul! how
blessed is that that now looketh upon thee!" And as I said these words,
with a painful anguish of sobbing and another prayer unto Death, a
young and gentle lady, who had been standing beside me where I lay,
conceiving that I wept and cried out because of the pain of mine infir-
mity, was taken with trembling and began to shed tears. Whereby other
ladies, who were about the room, becoming aware of my discomfort by
reason of the moan that she made, (who indeed was of my very near
kindred,) led her away from where I was, and then set themselves to
awaken me, thinking that I dreamed, and saying: "Sleep no longer, and
be not disquieted." Then, by their words, this strong imagination was
brought suddenly to an end, at the moment that I was about to say, "O
Beatrice! peace be with thee!" And already I had said, "O Beatrice!"
when being aroused, I opened mine eyes, and knew that it had been a
deception. But albeit I had indeed uttered her name, yet my voice was

so broken with sobs, that it was not understood by these ladies; so that
in spite of the sore shame that I felt, I turned towards them by Love's
counselling. And when they beheld me, they began to say, "He
seemeth as one dead," and to whisper among themselves, "Let us strive
if we may not comfort him." Whereupon they spake to me many sooth-
ing words, and questioned me moreover touching the cause of my fear.
Then I, being somewhat reassured, and having perceived that it was a
mere phantasy, said unto them, "This thing it was that made me
afeard"; and told them of all that I had seen, from the beginning even
unto the end, but without once speaking the name of my lady. Also,
after I had recovered from my sickness, I bethought me to write these
things in rhyme; deeming it a lovely thing to be known. Whereof I
wrote this poem:

> A very pitiful lady, very young,
>> Exceeding rich in human sympathies,
>> Stood by, what time I clamour'd upon Death;
>> And at the wild words wandering on my tongue
>> And at the piteous look within mine eyes
>> She was affrighted, that sobs choked her breath.
>> So by her weeping where I lay beneath,
>> Some other gentle ladies came to know
>> My state, and made her go:
>
> Afterward, bending themselves over me,
> One said, "Awaken thee!"
> And one, "What thing thy sleep disquieteth?"
> With that, my soul woke up from its eclipse,
> The while my lady's name rose to my lips:
>
> But utter'd in a voice so sob-broken,
>> So feeble with the agony of tears,
>> That I alone might hear it in my heart;
>> And though that look was on my visage then
>> Which he who is ashamed so plainly wears,
>> Love made that I through shame held not apart,
>> But gazed upon them. And my hue was such
>> That they look'd at each other and thought of death;
>> Saying under their breath
>> Most tenderly, "Oh, let us comfort him":
>> Then unto me: "What dream
>> Was thine, that it hath shaken thee so much?"
>> And when I was a little comforted,
>> "This, ladies, was the dream I dreamt," I said.

"I was a-thinking how life fails with us
  Suddenly after such a little while;
  When Love sobb'd in my heart, which is his home.
  Whereby my spirit wax'd so dolorous
  That in myself I said, with sick recoil:
  'Yea, to my lady too this Death must come.'
  And therewithal such a bewilderment
  Possess'd me, thath I shut mine eyes for peace;
  And in my brain did cease
  Order of thought, and every healthful thing.
  Afterwards, wandering
  Amid a swarm of doubts that came and went,
  Some certain women's faces hurried by,
  And shriek'd to me, 'Thou too shalt die, shalt die!'

"Then saw I many broken hinted sights
  In the uncertain state I stepp'd into.
  Meseem'd to be I know not in what place,
  Where ladies through the street, like mournful lights,
  Ran with loose hair, and eyes that frighten'd you
  By their own terror, and a pale amaze:
  The while, little by little, as I thought,
  The sun ceased, and the stars began to gather,
  And each wept at the other;
  And birds dropp'd in mid-flight out of the sky
  And earth shook suddenly;
  And I was 'ware of one, hoarse and tired out,
  Who ask'd of me: 'Hast thou not heard it said? . . .
  The lady, she that was so fair, is dead.'

"Then lifting up mine eyes, as the tears came,
  I saw the Angels, like a rain of manna,
  In a long flight flying back heavenward;
  Having a little cloud in front of them,
  After the which they went and said, 'Hosanna!'
  And if they had said more, you should have heard.
  Then Love spoke thus: 'Now all shall be made clear:
  Come and behold our lady where she lies.'
  These idle phantasies
  Then carried me to see my lady dead:
  And standing at her head
  Her ladies put a white veil over her;
  And with her was such very humbleness
  That she appeared to say, 'I am at peace.'

"And I became so humble in my grief,
  Seeing in her such deep humility,
  That I said: 'Death, I hold thee passing good
  Henceforth, and a most gentle sweet relief,
  Since my dear love has chosen to dwell with thee:
  Pity, not hate, is thine, well understood.
  Lo! I do so desire to see thy face
  That I am like as one who nears the tomb;
  My soul entreats thee, Come.'
  Then I departed, having made my moan;
  And when I was alone
  I said, and cast my eyes to the High Place:
  'Blessed is he, fair soul, who meets thy glance!'
  . . . . Just then you woke me, of your complaisaunce."

This poem has two parts. In the first, speaking to a person undefined, I tell how I was aroused from a vain phantasy by certain ladies, and how I promised them to tell what it was. In the second, I say how I told them. The second part begins here, "I was a-thinking." The first part divides into two. In the first, I tell that which certain ladies, and which one singly, did and said because of my phantasy, before I had returned into my right senses. In the second, I tell what these ladies said to me after I had left off this wandering: and it begins here, "But uttered in a voice." Then, when I say, "I was a-thinking," I say how I told them this my imagination; and concerning this I have two parts. In the first, I tell, in order, this imagination. In the second, saying at what time they called me, I covertly thank them: and this part begins here, "Just then you woke me."

XXIV

After this empty imagining, it happened on a day, as I sat thoughtful, that I was taken with such a strong trembling at the heart, that it could not have been otherwise in the presence of my lady. Whereupon I perceived that there was an appearance of Love beside me, and I seemed to see him coming from my lady; and he said, not aloud, but within my heart: "Now take heed that thou bless the day when I entered into thee; for it is fitting that thou shouldst do so." And with that my heart was so full of gladness, that I could hardly believe it to be of very truth mine own heart and not another. A short while after these words which my heart spoke to me with the tongue of Love, I saw coming towards me a certain lady who was very famous for her beauty, and of whom that friend whom I have already called the first among my friends had long been enamoured. This lady's right name was Joan; but because of her comeliness (or at least it was so imagined) she was called of many *Primavera* (Spring), and went by that name among them. Then looking again, I perceived that the most noble Beatrice followed after her. And when both these ladies had passed by me, it seemed to me that Love spake again in my heart, saying: "She that came first was called Spring, only because of that which was to happen on this day. And it was I myself who caused that name to be given her; seeing that as the Spring cometh first in the year, so should she come first on this day, when Beatrice was to show herself after the vision of her servant. And even if thou go about to consider her right name, it is also as one should say, 'She shall come first'; inasmuch as her name, Joan, is taken from that John who went before the True Light, saying: 'I am the voice of one crying in the wilderness: Prepare ye the way of the Lord.'" And also it seemed to me that he added other words, to wit: "He who should inquire delicately touching this matter, could not but call Beatrice by mine own name, which is to say, Love; beholding her so like unto me." Then I, having thought of this, imagined to write it with rhymes and send it unto my chief friend; but setting aside certain words which seemed proper to be set aside, because I believed that his heart still regarded the beauty of her that was called Spring. And I wrote this sonnet:

> I felt a spirit of love begin to stir
>   Within my heart, long time unfelt till then;
>   And saw Love coming towards me, fair and fain,
>   (That I scarce knew him for his joyful cheer,)
> Saying, "Be now indeed my worshipper!"
>   And in his speech he laugh'd and laugh'd again.
>   Then, while it was his pleasure to remain,
>   I chanced to look the way he had drawn near,
> And saw the Ladies Joan and Beatrice
>   Approach me, this the other following,
>   One and a second marvel instantly.
> And even as now my memory speaketh this,
>   Love spake it then: "The first it christen'd Spring;
>   The second Love, she is so like to me."

This sonnet has many parts: whereof the first tells how I felt awakened within my heart the accustomed tremor, and how it seemed that Love appeared to me joyful from afar. The second says how it appeared to me that Love spake within my heart, and what was his aspect. The third tells how, after he had in such wise been with me a space, I saw and heard certain things. The second part begins here, "Saying, 'Be now'"; the third here,

"Then, while it was his pleasure." The third part divides into two. In the first, I say what I saw. In the second, I say what I heard: and it begins here, "Love spake it then."

XXV

It might be here objected unto me, (and even by one worthy of controversy,) that I have spoken of Love as though it were a thing outward and visible: not only a spiritual essence, but as a bodily substance also. The which thing, in absolute truth, is a fallacy; Love not being of itself a substance, but an accident of substance. Yet that I speak of Love as though it were a thing tangible and even human, appears by three things which I say thereof. And firstly, I say that I perceived Love coming towards me; whereby, seeing that *to come* bespeaks locomotion, and seeing also how philosophy teacheth us that none but a corporeal substance hath locomotion, it seemeth that I speak of Love as of a corporeal substance. And secondly, I say that Love smiled; and thirdly, that Love spake; faculties (and especially the risible faculty) which appear proper unto man: whereby it further seemeth that I speak of Love as of a man. Now that this matter may be explained, (as is fitting,) it must first be remembered that anciently they who wrote poems of Love wrote not in the vulgar tongue, but rather certain poets in the Latin tongue. I mean, among us, although perchance the same may have been among others, and although likewise, as among the Greeks, they were not writers of spoken language, but men of letters, treated of these things. And indeed it is not a great number of years since poetry began to be made in the vulgar tongue; the writing of rhymes in spoken language corresponding to the writing in metre of Latin verse, by a certain analogy. And I say that it is but a little while, because if we examine the language of *oco* and the language of *sì* we shall not find in those tongues any written thing of an earlier date than the last hundred and fifty years. Also the reason why certain of a very mean sort obtained at the first some fame as poets is, that before them no man had written verses in the language of *sì*: and of these, the first was moved to the writing of such verses by the wish to make himself understood of a certain lady, unto whom Latin poetry was difficult. This thing is against such as rhyme concerning other matters than love; that mode of speech having been first used for the expression of love alone. Wherefore seeing that poets have a licence allowed them that is not allowed unto the writers of prose, and seeing also that they who write in rhyme are simply poets in the vulgar tongue, it becomes fitting and reasonable that a larger licence should be given to these than to other modern writers; and that any metaphor or rhetorical similitude which is permitted unto poets, should also be counted not unseemly in the rhymers of the vulgar tongue. Thus, if we perceive that the former

have caused inanimate things to speak as though they had sense and rea-
son, and to discourse one with another; yea, and not only actual things,
but such also as have no real existence, (seeing that they have made
things which are not, to speak; and oftentimes written of those which are
merely accidents as though they were substances and things human;) it
should therefore be permitted to the latter to do the like; which is to say,
not inconsiderately, but with such sufficient motive as may afterwards be
set forth in prose. That the Latin poets have done thus, appears through
Virgil, where he saith that Juno (to wit, a goddess hostile to the Trojans)
spake unto Æolus, master of the Winds; as it is written in the first book
of the Æneid, "*Æole, namque tibi*" etc.; and that this master of the Winds
made reply: "*Tuus, o regina, quid optes Explorare labor; mihi iussa
capessere fas est.*" And through the same poet, the inanimate thing
speaketh unto the animate, in the third book of the Æneid, where it is
written: "*Dardanidæ duri*" etc. With Lucan, the animate thing speaketh
to the inanimate; as thus: "*Multum, Roma, tamen debes civilibus armis.*"
In Horace man is made to speak to his own intelligence as unto another
person; (and not only hath Horace done this, but herein he followeth the
excellent Homer,) as thus in his Poetics: "*Dic mihi, Musa, virum*" etc.
Through Ovid, Love speaketh as a human creature in the beginning of
his discourse *De Remediis Amoris*, as thus: "*Bella mihi, video, bella
parantur, ait.*" By which ensamples* this thing shall be made manifest
unto such as may be offended at any part of this my book. And lest some
of the common sort should be moved to jeering hereat, I will here add,
that neither did these ancient poets speak thus without consideration, nor
should they who are makers of rhyme in our day write after the same
fashion, having no reason in what they write; for it were a shameful thing
if one should rhyme under the semblance of metaphor or rhetorical
similitude, and afterwards, being questioned thereof, should be unable to
rid his words of such semblance, unto their right understanding. Of
whom, (to wit, of such as rhyme thus foolishly,) myself and the first
among my friends do know many.

XXVI

But returning to the matter of my discourse. This excellent lady, of
whom I spake in what hath gone before, came at last into such favour
with all men, that when she passed anywhere folk ran to behold her;
which thing was a deep joy to me: and when she drew near unto any,
so much truth and simpleness entered into his heart, that he dared nei-
ther to lift his eyes nor to return her salutation: and unto this, many
who have felt it can bear witness. She went along crowned and clothed

---

*"ensample": example (ed.)

with humility, showing no whit of pride in all that she heard and saw: and when she had gone by, it was said of many, "This is not a woman, but one of the beautiful angels of Heaven!" and there were some that said: "This is surely a miracle; blessed be the Lord, who hath power to work thus marvellously." I say, of very sooth, that she showed herself so gentle and so full of all perfection, that she bred in those who looked upon her a soothing quiet beyond any speech; neither could any look upon her without sighing immediately. These things, and things yet more wonderful, were brought to pass through her miraculous virtue. Wherefore I, considering thereof and wishing to resume the endless tale of her praises, resolved to write somewhat wherein I might dwell on her surpassing influence; to the end that not only they who had beheld her, but others also, might know as much concerning her as words could give to the understanding. And it was then that I wrote this sonnet:

> My lady looks so gentle and so pure
>   When yielding salutation by the way,
>   That the tongue trembles and has nought to say,
>   And the eyes, which fain would see, may not endure.
> And still, amid the praise she hears secure,
>   She walks with humbleness for her array;
>   Seeming a creature sent from Heaven to stay
>   On earth, and show a miracle made sure.
> She is so pleasant in the eyes of men
>   That through the sight the inmost heart doth gain
>   A sweetness which needs proof to know it by:
> And from between her lips there seems to move
>   A soothing spirit that is full of love,
>   Saying for ever to the soul, "O sigh!"

This sonnet is so easy to understand, from what is afore narrated, that it needs no division: and therefore, leaving it,

XXVII

I say also that this excellent lady came into such favour with all men, that not only she herself was honoured and commended; but through her companionship, honour and commendation came unto others. Wherefore I, perceiving this and wishing that it should also be made manifest to those that beheld it not, wrote the sonnet here following; wherein is signified the power which her virtue had upon other ladies:

> For certain he hath seen all perfectness
>   Who among other ladies hath seen mine:

They that go with her humbly should combine
    To thank their God for such peculiar grace.
So perfect is the beauty of her face
    That it begets in no wise any sign
    Of envy, but draws round her a clear line
Of love, and blessed faith, and gentleness.
Merely the sight of her makes all things bow:
    Not she herself alone is holier
    Than all; but hers, through her, are raised above.
From all her acts such lovely graces flow
    That truly one may never think of her
    Without a passion of exceeding love.

This sonnet has three parts. In the first, I say in what company this lady appeared most wondrous. In the second, I say how gracious was her society. In the third, I tell of the things which she, with power, worked upon others. The second begins here, "They that go with her"; the third here, "So perfect." This last part divides into three. In the first, I tell what she operated upon women, that is, by their own faculties. In the second, I tell what she operated in them through others. In the third, I say how she not only operated in women, but in all people; and not only while herself present, but, by memory of her, operated wondrously. The second begins here, "Merely the sight"; the third here, "From all her acts."

XXVIII

Thereafter on a day, I began to consider that which I had said of my lady: to wit, in these two sonnets aforegone: and becoming aware that I had not spoken of her immediate effect on me at that especial time, it seemed to me that I had spoken defectively. Whereupon I resolved to write somewhat of the manner wherein I was then subject to her influence, and of what her influence then was. And conceiving that I should not be able to say these things in the small compass of a sonnet, I began therefore a poem with this beginning:

Long hath so long possess'd me for his own
    And made his lordship so familiar
    That he, who at first irk'd me, is now grown
Unto my heart as its best secrets are.
    And thus, when he in such sore wise doth mar
My life that all its strength seems gone from it,
Mine inmost being then feels thoroughly quit
Of anguish, and all evil keeps afar.
Love also gathers to such power in me
That my sighs speak, each one a grievous thing.

Always soliciting
My lady's salutation piteously.
Whenever she beholds me, it is so,
Who is more sweet than any words can show.

XXIX

"How doth the city sit solitary, that was full of people! how is she become a widow!"

I was still occupied with this poem, (having composed thereof only the above-written stanza,) when the Lord God of justice called my most gracious lady unto Himself, that she might be glorious under the banner of that blessed Queen Mary, whose name had always a deep reverence in the words of holy Beatrice. And because haply it might be found good that I should say somewhat concerning her departure, I will herein declare what are the reasons which make that I shall not do so. And the reasons are three. The first is, that such matter belongeth not of right to the present argument, if one consider the opening of this little book. The second is, that even though the present argument required it, my pen doth not suffice to write in a fit manner of this thing. And the third is, that were it both possible and of absolute necessity, it would still be unseemly for me to speak thereof, seeing that thereby it must behove me to speak also mine own praises: a thing that in whosoever doeth it is worthy of blame. For the which reasons, I will leave this matter to be treated of by some other than myself. Nevertheless, as the number nine, which number hath often had mention in what hath gone before, (and not, as it might appear, without reason,) seems also to have borne a part in the manner of her death: it is therefore right that I should say somewhat thereof. And for this cause, having first said what was the part it bore herein, I will afterwards point out a reason which made that this number was so closely allied unto my lady.

XXX

I say, then, that according to the division of time in [Arabia],* her most noble spirit departed from among us in the first hour of the ninth day of the month; and according to the division of time in Syria, in the ninth month of the year; seeing that Tismim, which with us is October, is there the first month. Also she was taken from among us in that year of our reckoning (to wit, of the years of our Lord) in which the perfect number was nine times multiplied within that century wherein she was born into the world: which is to say, the thirteenth century of

---

*Scholars have noted that Rossetti incorrectly translated this reference as in "Italy." (ed.)

Christians. And touching the reason why this number was so closely al-
lied unto her, it may peradventure be this. According to Ptolemy, (and
also to the Christian verity,) the revolving heavens are nine; and ac-
cording to the common opinion among astrologers, these nine heavens
together have influence over the earth. Wherefore it would appear that
this number was thus allied unto her for the purpose of signifying that,
at her birth, all these nine heavens were at perfect unity with each other
as to their influence. This is one reason that may be brought: but more
narrowly considering, and according to the infallible truth, this num-
ber was her own self: that is to say by similitude. As thus. The number
three is the root of the number nine; seeing that without the interposi-
tion of any other number, being multiplied merely by itself, it pro-
duceth nine, as we manifestly perceive that three times three are nine.
Thus, three being of itself the efficient of nine, and the Great Efficient
of Miracles being of Himself Three Persons (to wit: the Father, the Son,
and the Holy Spirit), which, being Three, are also One:—this lady was
accompanied by the number nine to the end that men might clearly
perceive her to be a nine, that is, a miracle, whose only root is the Holy
Trinity. It may be that a more subtile person would find for this thing a
reason of greater subtilty: but such is the reason that I find, and that
liketh me best.

XXXI

After this most gracious creature had gone out from among us, the
whole city came to be as it were widowed and despoiled of all dignity.
Then I, left mourning in this desolate city, wrote unto the principal per-
sons thereof, in an epistle, concerning its condition; taking for my com-
mencement those words of Jeremias: "How doth the city sit solitary!"
And I make mention of this, that none may marvel wherefore I set
down these words before, in beginning to treat of her death. Also if any
should blame me, in that I do not transcribe that epistle whereof I have
spoken, I will make it mine excuse that I began this little book with the
intent that it should be written altogether in the vulgar tongue; where-
fore, seeing that the epistle I speak of is in Latin, it belongeth not to
mine undertaking: more especially as I know that my chief friend, for
whom I write this book, wished also that the whole of it should be in
the vulgar tongue.

XXXII

When mine eyes had wept for some while, until they were so weary
with weeping that I could no longer through them give ease to my sor-
row, I bethought me that a few mournful words might stand me instead
of tears. And therefore I proposed to make a poem, that weeping I

might speak therein of her for whom so much sorrow had destroyed my spirit; and then I began "The eyes that weep."

That this poem may seem to remain the more widowed at its close, I will divide it before writing it; and this method I will observe henceforward. I say that this poor little poem has three parts. The first is a prelude. In the second, I speak of her. In the third, I speak pitifully to the poem. The second begins here, "Beatrice is gone up"; the third here, "Weep, pitiful Song of mine." The first divides into three. In the first, I say what moves me to speak. In the second, I say to whom I mean to speak. In the third, I say of whom I mean to speak. The second begins here, "And because often, thinking"; the third here, "And I will say." Then, when I say, "Beatrice is gone up," I speak of her; and concerning this I have two parts. First, I tell the cause why she was taken away from us: afterwards, I say how one weeps her parting; and this part commences here, "Wonderfully." This part divides into three. In the first, I say who it is that weeps her not. In the second, I say who it is that doth weep her. In the third, I speak of my condition. The second begins here, "But sighing comes, and grief"; the third, "With sighs." Then, when I say, "Weep, pitiful Song of mine," I speak to this my song, telling it what ladies to go to, and stay with.

> The eyes that weep for pity of the heart
> Have wept so long that their grief languisheth
> And they have no more tears to weep withal:
> And now, if I would ease me of a part
> Of what, little by little, leads to death,
> It must be done by speech, or not at all.
> And because often, thinking, I recall
> How it was pleasant, ere she went afar,
> To talk of her with you, kind damozels,
> I talk with no one else,
> But only with such hearts as women's are.
> And I will say—still sobbing as speech fails—
> That she hath gone to Heaven suddenly,
> And hath left Love below, to mourn with me.
>
> Beatrice is gone up into high Heaven,
> The kingdom where the angels are at peace;
> And lives with them; and to her friends is dead.
> Not by the frost of winter was she driven
> Away, like others; nor by summer-heats;
> But through a perfect gentleness, instead.
> For from the lamp of her meek lowlihead*

---

*"lowlihead": humility (ed.)

Such an exceeding glory went up hence
That it woke wonder in the Eternal Sire,
Until a sweet desire
Enter'd Him for that lovely excellence,
So that He bade her to Himself aspire:
Counting this weary and most evil place
Unworthy of a thing so full of grace.

Wonderfully out of the beautiful form
Soar'd her clear spirit, waxing glad the while;
And is in its first home, there where it is.
Who speaks thereof, and feels not the tears warm
Upon his face, must have become so vile
As to be dead to all sweet sympathies.
Out upon him! an abject wretch like this
May not imagine anything of her—
He needs no bitter tears for his relief.
But sighing comes, and grief,
And the desire to find no comforter,
(Save only Death, who makes all sorrow brief,)
To him who for a while turns in his thought
How she hath been among us, and is not.

With sighs my bosom always laboureth
On thinking, as I do continually,
Of her for whom my heart now breaks apace;
And very often when I think of death,
Such a great inward longing comes to me
That it will change the colour of my face;
And, if the idea settles in its place,
All my limbs shake as with an ague-fit;
Till, starting up in wild bewilderment,
I do become so shent*
That I go forth, lest folk misdoubt of it.
Afterward, calling with a sore lament
On Beatrice, I ask, "Canst thou be dead?"
And calling on her, I am comforted.

Grief with its tears, and anguish with its sighs
Come to me now whene'er I am alone;
So that I think the sight of me gives pain.
And what my life hath been, that living dies,

---

*"shent": ruined, lost (ed.)

Since for my lady the New Birth's begun,
I have not any language to explain.
And so, dear ladies, though my heart were fain,
I scarce could tell indeed how I am thus.
All joy is with my bitter life at war;
Yea, I am fallen so far
That all men seem to say, "Go out from us,"
Eyeing my cold white lips, how dead they are.
But she, though I be bow'd unto the dust,
Watches me; and will guerdon me, I trust.

Weep, pitiful Song of mine, upon they way,
To the dames going, and the damozels,
For whom, and for none else,
Thy sisters have made music many a day.
Thou, that art very sad and not as they,
Go dwell thou with them as a mourner dwells.

XXXIII

After I had written this poem, I received the visit of a friend whom I counted as second unto me in the degrees of friendship, and who, moreover, had been united by the nearest kindred to that most gracious creature. And when we had a little spoken together, he began to solicit me that I would write somewhat in memory of a lady who had died; and he disguised his speech, so as to seem to be speaking of another who was but lately dead: wherefore I, perceiving that his speech was of none other than that blessed one herself, told him that it should be done as he required. Then afterwards, having thought thereof, I imagined to give vent in a sonnet to some part of my hidden lamentations: but in such sort that it might seem to be spoken by this friend of mine, to whom I was to give it. And the sonnet saith thus: "Stay now with me," etc.

This sonnet has two parts. In the first, I call the Faithful of Love to hear me. In the second, I relate my miserable condition. The second begins here, "Mark how they force."

Stay now with me, and listen to my sighs,
    Ye piteous hearts, as pity bids ye do.
    Mark how they force their way out and press through;
    If they be once pent up, the whole life dies.
Seeing that now indeed my weary eyes
    Oftener refuse than I can tell to you,
    (Even though my endless grief is ever new,)
    To weep, and let the smother'd anguish rise.
Also in sighing ye shall hear me call

On her whose blessed presence doth enrich
　　The only home that well befitteth her:
And ye shall hear a bitter scorn of all
　　Sent from the inmost of my spirit in speech
　　That mourns its joy and its joy's minister.

XXXIV

But when I had written this sonnet, bethinking me who he was to whom I was to give it, that it might appear to be his speech, it seemed to me that this was but a poor and barren gift for one of her so near kindred. Wherefore, before giving him this sonnet, I wrote two stanzas of a poem: the first being written in very sooth as though it were spoken by him, but the other being mine own speech, albeit, unto one who should not look closely, they would both seem to be said by the same person. Nevertheless, looking closely, one must perceive that it is not so, inasmuch as one does not call this most gracious creature *his lady*, and the other does, as is manifestly apparent. And I gave the poem and the sonnet unto my friend, saying that I had made them only for him.

The poem begins, "Whatever while," and has two parts. In the first, that is, in the first stanza, this my dear friend, her kinsman, laments. In the second, I lament; that is, in the other stanza, which begins, "For ever." And thus it appears that in this poem two persons lament, of whom one laments as a brother, the other as a servant.

Whatever while the thought comes over me
　　That I may not again
　　Behold that lady whom I mourn for now,
About my heart my mind brings constantly
　　So much of extreme pain
That I say: "Soul of mine, why stayest thou?
Truly the anguish, Soul, that we must bow
Beneath, until we win out of this life,
　　Gives me full oft a fear that trembleth:
　　So that I call on Death
Even as on Sleep one calleth after strife,
Saying: 'Come unto me. Life showeth grim
And bare; and if one dies, I envy him.'"

For ever, among all my sighs which burn,
　　There is a piteous speech
　　That clamours upon Death continually:
Yea, unto him doth my whole spirit turn
　　Since first his hand did reach
My lady's life with most foul cruelty.

But from the height of woman's fairness, she,
Going up from us with the joy we had,
Grew perfectly and spiritually fair;
That so she spreads even there
A light of Love which makes the Angels glad,
And even unto their subtle minds can bring
A certain awe of profound marvelling.

XXXV

On that day which fulfilled the year since my lady had been made of the citizens of eternal life, remembering me of her as I sat alone, I betook myself to draw the resemblance of an angel upon certain tablets. And while I did thus, chancing to turn my head, I perceived that some were standing beside me to whom I should have given courteous welcome, and that they were observing what I did: also I learned afterwards that they had been there a while before I perceived them. Perceiving whom, I arose for salutation, and said: "Another was with me." Afterwards, when they had left me, I set myself again to mine occupation, to wit, to the drawing figures of angels: in doing which, I conceived to write of this matter in rhyme, as for her anniversary, and to address my rhymes unto those who had just left me. It was then that I wrote the sonnet which saith, "That lady": and as this sonnet hath two commencements, it behoveth me to divide it with both of them here.

I say that, according to the first, this sonnet has three parts. In the first, I say that this lady was then in my memory. In the second, I tell what Love therefore did with me. In the third, I speak of the effects of Love. The second begins here, "Love, knowing"; the third here, "Forth went they." This part divides into two. In the one, I say that all my sighs issued speaking. In the other, I say how some spoke certain words different from the others. The second begins here, "And still." In this same manner is it divided with the other beginning, save that, in the first part, I tell when this lady had thus come into my mind, and this I say not in the other.

FIRST COMMENCEMENT
That lady of all gentle memories
Had lighted on my soul;—whose new abode
Lies now, as it was well ordain'd of God,
Among the poor in heart, where Mary is.

SECOND COMMENCEMENT
That lady of all gentle memories
Had lighted on my soul;—for whose sake flow'd
The tears of Love; in whom the power abode
Which led you to observe while I did this.

Love, knowing that dear image to be his,
  Woke up within the sick heart sorrow-bow'd,
  Unto the sighs which are its weary load,
  Saying, "Go forth." And they went forth, I wis;
Forth went they from my breast that throbb'd and ached;
  With such a pang as oftentimes will bathe
  Mine eyes with tears when I am left alone.
And still those sighs which drew the heaviest breath
  Came whispering thus: "O noble intellect!
  It is a year to-day that thou art gone."

XXXVI

Then, having sat for some space sorely in thought because of the time that was now past, I was so filled with dolorous imaginings that it became outwardly manifest in mine altered countenance. Whereupon, feeling this and being in dread lest any should have seen me, I lifted mine eyes to look; and then perceived a young and very beautiful lady, who was gazing upon me from a window with a gaze full of pity, so that the very sum of pity appeared gathered together in her. And seeing that unhappy persons, when they beget compassion in others, are then most moved unto weeping, as though they also felt pity for themselves, it came to pass that mine eyes began to be inclined unto tears. Wherefore, becoming fearful lest I should make manifest mine abject condition, I rose up, and went where I could not be seen of that lady; saying afterwards within myself: "Certainly with her also must abide most noble Love." And with that, I resolved upon writing a sonnet, wherein, speaking unto her, I should say all that I have just said. And as this sonnet is very evident, I will not divide it.

Mine eyes beheld the blessed pity spring
  Into thy countenance immediately
  A while agone, when thou beheld'st in me
  The sickness only hidden grief can bring;
And then I knew thou wast considering
  How abject and forlorn my life must be;
  And I became afraid that thou shouldst see
  My weeping, and account it a base thing.
Therefore I went out from thee; feeling how
  The tears were straightway loosen'd at my heart
  Beneath thine eyes' compassionate control.
And afterwards I said within my soul:
  "Lo! with this lady dwells the counterpart
  Of the same Love who holds me weeping now."

XXXVII

It happened after this, that whensoever I was seen of this lady, she became pale and of a piteous countenance, as though it had been with love; whereby she remembered me many times of my own most noble lady, who was wont to be of a like paleness. And I know that often, when I could not weep nor in any way give ease unto mine anguish, I went to look upon this lady, who seemed to bring the tears into my eyes by the mere sight of her. Of the which thing I bethought me to speak unto her in rhyme, and then made this sonnet: which begins, "Love's pallor," and which is plain without being divided, by its exposition aforesaid.

> Love's pallor and the semblance of deep ruth
>   Were never yet shown forth so perfectly
>   In any lady's face, chancing to see
>   Grief's miserable countenance uncouth,
> As in thine, lady, they have sprung to soothe,
>   When in mine anguish thou hast look'd on me;
>   Until sometimes it seems as if, through thee,
>   My heart might almost wander from its truth.
> Yet so it is, I cannot hold mine eyes
>   From gazing very often upon thine
>   In the sore hope to shed those tears they keep;
> And at such time, thou mak'st the pent tears rise
>   Even to the brim, till the eyes waste and pine;
>   Yet cannot they, while thou art present, weep.

XXXVIII

At length, by the constant sight of this lady mine eyes began to be gladdened overmuch with her company; through which thing many times I had much unrest, and rebuked myself as a base person: also, many times I cursed the unsteadfastness of mine eyes, and said to them inwardly: "Was not your grievous condition of weeping wont one while to make others weep? And will ye now forget this thing because a lady looketh upon you? who so looketh merely in compassion of the grief ye then showed for your own blessed lady. But whatso ye can, that do ye, accursed eyes! many a time will I make you remember it! for never, till death dry you up, should ye make an end of your weeping." And when I had spoken thus unto mine eyes, I was taken again with extreme and grievous sighing. And to the end that this inward strife which I had undergone might not be hidden from all saving the miserable wretch who endured it, I proposed to write a sonnet, and to comprehend in it this horrible condition. And I wrote this which begins "The very bitter weeping."

The sonnet has two parts. In the first, I speak to my eyes, as my heart spoke within myself. In the second, I remove a difficulty, showing who it is that speaks thus: and this part begins here, "So far." It well might receive other divisions also; but this would be useless, since it is manifest by the preceding exposition.

"The very bitter weeping that ye made
    So long a time together, eyes of mine,
    Was wont to make the tears of pity shine
    In other eyes full oft, as I have said.
But now this thing were scarce rememberèd
    If I, on my part, foully would combine
    With you, and not recall each ancient sign
    Of grief, and her for whom your tears were shed.
It is your fickleness that doth betray
    My mind to fears, and makes me tremble thus
    What while a lady greets me with her eyes.
Except by death, we must not any way
    Forget our lady who is gone from us."
    So far doth my heart utter, and then sighs.

XXXIX

The sight of this lady brought me into so unwonted a condition that I often thought of her as of one too dear unto me; and I began to consider her thus: "This lady is young, beautiful, gentle, and wise: perchance it was Love himself who set her in my path, that so my life might find peace." And there were times when I thought yet more fondly, until my heart consented unto its reasoning. But when it had so consented, my thought would often turn round upon me, as moved by reason, and cause me to say within myself: "What hope is this which would console me after so base a fashion, and which hath taken the place of all other imagining?" Also there was another voice within me, that said: "And wilt thou, having suffered so much tribulation through Love, not escape while yet thou mayest from so much bitterness? Thou must surely know that this thought carries with it the desire of Love, and drew its life from the gentle eyes of that lady who vouchsafed thee so much pity." Wherefore I, having striven sorely and very often with myself, bethought me to say somewhat thereof in rhyme. And seeing that in the battle of doubts, the victory most often remained with such as inclined towards the lady of whom I speak, it seemed to me that I should address this sonnet unto her: in the first line whereof, I call that thought which spake of her a gentle thought, only because it spoke of one who was gentle; being of itself most vile.

In this sonnet I make myself into two, according as my thoughts were divided one from the other. The one part I call Heart, that is, appetite; the other, Soul, that is, reason; and I tell what one saith to the other. And that it is fitting to call the appetite Heart, and the reason Soul, is manifest enough to them to whom I wish this to be open. True it is that, in the preceding sonnet, I take the part of the Heart against the Eyes; and that appears contrary to what I say in the present; and therefore I say that, there also, by the Heart I mean appetite, because yet greater was my desire to remember my most gentle lady than to see this other, although indeed I had some appetite towards her, but it appeared slight: wherefore it appears that the one statement is not contrary to the other. This sonnet has three parts. In the first, I begin to say to this lady how my desires turn all towards her. In the second, I say how the Soul, that is, the reason, speaks to the Heart, that is, to the appetite. In the third, I say how the latter answers. The second begins here, "And what is this?" the third here, "And the heart answers."

> A gentle thought there is will often start,
>   Within my secret self, to speech of thee;
>   Also of Love it speaks so tenderly
>   That much in me consents and takes its part.
> "And what is this," the soul saith to the heart,
>   "That cometh thus to comfort thee and me,
>   And thence where it would dwell, thus potently
>   Can drive all other thoughts by its strange art?"
> And the heart answers: "Be no more at strife
>   'Twixt doubt and doubt: this is Love's messenger
>   And speaketh but his words, from him received;
> And all the strength it owns and all the life
>   It draweth from the gentle eyes of her
>   Who, looking on our grief, hath often grieved."

XL

But against this adversary of reason, there rose up in me on a certain day, about [noon],* a strong visible phantasy, wherein I seemed to behold the most gracious Beatrice, habited in that crimson raiment which she had worn when I had first beheld her; also she appeared to me of the same tender age as then. Whereupon I fell into a deep thought of her: and my memory ran back according to the order of

---

*Scholars have noted that Rossetti incorrectly translated this reference as the "ninth hour." (ed.)

time, unto all those matters in the which she had borne a part; and my heart began painfully to repent of the desire by which it had so basely let itself be possessed during so many days, contrary to the constancy of reason. And then, this evil desire being quite gone from me, all my thoughts turned again unto their excellent Beatrice. And I say most truly that from that hour I thought constantly of her with the whole humbled and ashamed heart; the which became often manifest in sighs, that had among them the name of that most gracious creature, and how she departed from us. Also it would come to pass very often, through the bitter anguish of some one thought, that I forgot both it, and myself, and where I was. By this increase of sighs, my weeping, which before had been somewhat lessened, increased in like manner; so that mine eyes seemed to long only for tears and to cherish them, and came at last to be circled about with red as though they had suffered martyrdom; neither were they able to look again upon the beauty of any face that might again bring them to shame and evil; from which things it will appear that they were fitly guerdoned for their unsteadfastness. Wherefore I, (wishing that mine abandonment of all such evil desires and vain temptations should be certified and made manifest, beyond all doubts which might have been suggested by the rhymes aforewritten,) proposed to write a sonnet, wherein I should express this purport. And I then wrote, "Woe's me!"

I said, "Woe's me!" because I was ashamed of the trifling of mine eyes. This sonnet I do not divide, since its purport is manifest enough.

Woe's me! by dint of all these sighs that come
    Forth of my heart, its endless grief to prove,
    Mine eyes are conquer'd, so that even to move
    Their lids for greeting is grown troublesome.
They wept so long that now they are grief's home
    And count their tears all laughter far above:
    They wept till they are circled now by Love
    With a red circle in sign of martyrdom.
These musings, and the sighs they bring from me,
    Are grown at last so constant and so sore
    That Love swoons in my spirit with faint breath;
Hearing in those sad sounds continually
    The most sweet name that my dear lady bore,
    With many grievous words touching her death.

XLI

About this time, it happened that a great number of persons undertook a pilgrimage, to the end that they might behold that blessed portraiture bequeathed unto us by our Lord Jesus Christ as the image of His beautiful countenance, (upon which countenance my dear lady now looketh continually). And certain among these pilgrims, who seemed very thoughtful, passed by a path which is wellnigh in the midst of the city where my most gracious lady was born, and abode, and at last died. Then I, beholding them, said within myself: "These pilgrims seem to be come from very far; and I think they cannot have heard speak of this lady, or know anything concerning her. Their thoughts are not of her, but of other things; it may be, of their friends who are far distant, and whom we, in our turn, know not." And I went on to say: "I know that if they were of a country near unto us, they would in some wise seem disturbed, passing through this city which is so full of grief." And I said also: "If I could speak with them a space, I am certain that I should make them weep before they went forth of this city; for those things that they would hear from me must needs beget weeping in any." And when the last of them had gone by me, I bethought me to write a sonnet, showing forth mine inward speech; and that it might seem the more pitiful, I made as though I had spoken it indeed unto them. And I wrote this sonnet, which beginneth: "Ye pilgrimfolk." I made use of the word *pilgrim* for its general signification; for "pilgrim" may be understood in two senses, one general, and one special. General, so far as any man may be called a pilgrim who leaveth the place of his birth; whereas, more narrowly speaking, he is only a pilgrim who goeth towards or frowards the House of St. James. For there are three separate denominations proper unto those who undertake journeys to the glory of God. They are called Palmers who go beyond the seas eastward, whence often they bring palm-branches. And Pilgrims, as I have said, are they who journey unto the holy House of Gallicia; seeing that no other apostle was buried so far from his birthplace as was the blessed Saint James. And there is a third sort who are called Romers; in that they go whither these whom I have called pilgrims went: which is to say, unto Rome.

This sonnet is not divided, because its own words sufficiently declare it.

    Ye pilgrim-folk, advancing pensively
        As if in thought of distant things, I pray,
        Is your own land indeed so far away
        As by your aspect it would seem to be—
    That nothing of our grief comes over ye
        Though passing through the mournful town midway;
        Like unto men that understand to-day
        Nothing at all of her great misery?

Yet if ye will but stay, whom I accost,
  And listen to my words a little space,
  At going ye shall mourn with a loud voice.
It is her Beatrice that she hath lost;
  Of whom the least word spoken holds such grace
  That men weep hearing it, and have no choice.

XLII

A while after these things, two gentle ladies sent unto me, praying
that I would bestow upon them certain of these my rhymes. And I, (tak-
ing into account their worthiness and consideration,) resolved that I
would write also a new thing, and send it them together with those oth-
ers, to the end that their wishes might be more honourably fulfilled.
Therefore I made a sonnet, which narrates my condition, and which I
caused to be conveyed to them, accompanied with the one preceding,
and with that other which begins, "Stay now with me and listen to my
sighs." And the new sonnet is, "Beyond the sphere."

*This sonnet comprises five parts. In the first, I tell whither my
thought goeth, naming the place by the name of one of its effects. In
the second, I say wherefore it goeth up, and who makes it go thus. In
the third, I tell what it saw, namely, a lady honoured. And I then call
it a "Pilgrim Spirit," because it goes up spiritually, and like a pilgrim
who is out of his known country. In the fourth, I say how the spirit sees
her such (that is, in such quality) that I cannot understand her; that is
to say, my thought rises into the quality of her in a degree that my in-
tellect cannot comprehend, seeing that our intellect is, towards those
blessed souls, like our eye weak against the sun; and this the
Philosopher says in the Second of the Metaphysics. In the fifth, I say
that, although I cannot see there whither my thought carries me—that
is, to her admirable essence—I at least understand this, namely, that it
is a thought of my lady, because I often hear her name therein. And at
the end of this fifth part, I say, "Ladies mine," to show that they are
ladies to whom I speak. The second part begins, "A new perception";
the third, "When it hath reached"; the fourth, "It sees her such"; the
fifth, "And yet I know." It might be divided yet more nicely, and made
yet clearer; but this division may pass, and therefore I stay not to divide
it further.*

Beyond the sphere which spreads to widest space
  Now soars the sigh that my heart sends above:
  A new perception born of grieving Love
  Guideth it upward the untrodden ways.

When it hath reach'd unto the end, and stays,
    It sees a lady round whom splendours move
    In homage; till, by the great light thereof
    Abash'd, the pilgrim spirit stands at gaze.
It sees her such, that when it tells me this
    Which it hath seen, I understand it not,
    It hath a speech so subtile and so fine.
And yet I know its voice within my thought
    Often remembereth me of Beatrice:
    So that I understand it, ladies mine.

XLIII

After writing this sonnet, it was given unto me to behold a very wonderful vision; wherein I saw things which determined me that I would say nothing further of this most blessed one, until such time as I could discourse more worthily concerning her. And to this end I labour all I can; as she well knoweth. Wherefore if it be His pleasure through whom is the life of all things, that my life continue with me a few years, it is my hope that I shall yet write concerning her what hath not before been written of any woman. After the which, may it seem good unto Him who is the Master of Grace, that my spirit should go hence to behold the glory of its lady; to wit, of that blessed Beatrice who now gazeth continually on His countenance, who is blessed throughout all ages.

POETRY

101 GREAT AMERICAN POEMS, Edited by The American Poetry & Literacy Project. (0-486-40158-8)

100 BEST-LOVED POEMS, Edited by Philip Smith. (0-486-28553-7)

ENGLISH ROMANTIC POETRY: An Anthology, Edited by Stanley Appelbaum. (0-486-29282-7)

THE INFERNO, Dante Alighieri. Translated and with notes by Henry Wadsworth Longfellow. (0-486-44288-8)

PARADISE LOST, John Milton. Introduction and Notes by John A. Himes. (0-486-44287-X)

SPOON RIVER ANTHOLOGY, Edgar Lee Masters. (0-486-27275-3)

SELECTED CANTERBURY TALES, Geoffrey Chaucer. (0-486-28241-4)

SELECTED POEMS, Emily Dickinson. (0-486-26466-1)

LEAVES OF GRASS: The Original 1855 Edition, Walt Whitman. (0-486-45676-5)

COMPLETE SONNETS, William Shakespeare. (0-486-26686-9)

THE RAVEN AND OTHER FAVORITE POEMS, Edgar Allan Poe. (0-486-26685-0)

ENGLISH VICTORIAN POETRY: An Anthology, Edited by Paul Negri. (0-486-40425-0)

SELECTED POEMS, Walt Whitman. (0-486-26878-0)

THE ROAD NOT TAKEN AND OTHER POEMS, Robert Frost. (0-486-27550-7)

AFRICAN-AMERICAN POETRY: An Anthology, 1773-1927, Edited by Joan R. Sherman. (0-486-29604-0)

GREAT SHORT POEMS, Edited by Paul Negri. (0-486-41105-2)

THE RIME OF THE ANCIENT MARINER, Samuel Taylor Coleridge. (0-486-27266-4)

THE WASTE LAND, PRUFROCK AND OTHER POEMS, T. S. Eliot. (0-486-40061-1)

SONG OF MYSELF, Walt Whitman. (0-486-41410-8)

AENEID, Vergil. (0-486-28749-1)

SONGS FOR THE OPEN ROAD: Poems of Travel and Adventure, Edited by The American Poetry & Literacy Project. (0-486-40646-6)

SONGS OF INNOCENCE AND SONGS OF EXPERIENCE, William Blake. (0-486-27051-3)

WORLD WAR ONE BRITISH POETS: Brooke, Owen, Sassoon, Rosenberg and Others, Edited by Candace Ward. (0-486-29568-0)

GREAT SONNETS, Edited by Paul Negri. (0-486-28052-7)

CHRISTMAS CAROLS: Complete Verses, Edited by Shane Weller. (0-486-27397-0)

FICTION

FLATLAND: A ROMANCE OF MANY DIMENSIONS, Edwin A. Abbott. (0-486-27263-X)

PRIDE AND PREJUDICE, Jane Austen. (0-486-28473-5)

CIVIL WAR SHORT STORIES AND POEMS, Edited by Bob Blaisdell. (0-486-48226-X)

THE DECAMERON: Selected Tales, Giovanni Boccaccio. Edited by Bob Blaisdell. (0-486-41113-3)

JANE EYRE, Charlotte Brontë. (0-486-42449-9)

WUTHERING HEIGHTS, Emily Brontë. (0-486-29256-8)

THE THIRTY-NINE STEPS, John Buchan. (0-486-28201-5)

ALICE'S ADVENTURES IN WONDERLAND, Lewis Carroll. (0-486-27543-4)

MY ÁNTONIA, Willa Cather. (0-486-28240-6)

THE AWAKENING, Kate Chopin. (0-486-27786-0)

HEART OF DARKNESS, Joseph Conrad. (0-486-26464-5)

LORD JIM, Joseph Conrad. (0-486-40650-4)

THE RED BADGE OF COURAGE, Stephen Crane. (0-486-26465-3)

THE WORLD'S GREATEST SHORT STORIES, Edited by James Daley. (0-486-44716-2)

A CHRISTMAS CAROL, Charles Dickens. (0-486-26865-9)

GREAT EXPECTATIONS, Charles Dickens. (0-486-41586-4)

A TALE OF TWO CITIES, Charles Dickens. (0-486-40651-2)

CRIME AND PUNISHMENT, Fyodor Dostoyevsky. Translated by Constance Garnett. (0-486-41587-2)

THE ADVENTURES OF SHERLOCK HOLMES, Sir Arthur Conan Doyle. (0-486-47491-7)

THE HOUND OF THE BASKERVILLES, Sir Arthur Conan Doyle. (0-486-28214-7)

BLAKE: PROPHET AGAINST EMPIRE, David V. Erdman. (0-486-26719-9)

WHERE ANGELS FEAR TO TREAD, E. M. Forster. (0-486-27791-7)

BEOWULF, Translated by R. K. Gordon. (0-486-27264-8)

THE RETURN OF THE NATIVE, Thomas Hardy. (0-486-43165-7)

THE SCARLET LETTER, Nathaniel Hawthorne. (0-486-28048-9)

SIDDHARTHA, Hermann Hesse. (0-486-40653-9)

THE ODYSSEY, Homer. (0-486-40654-7)

THE TURN OF THE SCREW, Henry James. (0-486-26684-2)

DUBLINERS, James Joyce. (0-486-26870-5)

FICTION

THE METAMORPHOSIS AND OTHER STORIES, Franz Kafka. (0-486-29030-1)

SONS AND LOVERS, D. H. Lawrence. (0-486-42121-X)

THE CALL OF THE WILD, Jack London. (0-486-26472-6)

GREAT AMERICAN SHORT STORIES, Edited by Paul Negri. (0-486-42119-8)

THE GOLD-BUG AND OTHER TALES, Edgar Allan Poe. (0-486-26875-6)

ANTHEM, Ayn Rand. (0-486-49277-X)

FRANKENSTEIN, Mary Shelley. (0-486-28211-2)

THE JUNGLE, Upton Sinclair. (0-486-41923-1)

THREE LIVES, Gertrude Stein. (0-486-28059-4)

THE STRANGE CASE OF DR. JEKYLL AND MR. HYDE, Robert Louis Stevenson. (0-486-26688-5)

DRACULA, Bram Stoker. (0-486-41109-5)

UNCLE TOM'S CABIN, Harriet Beecher Stowe. (0-486-44028-1)

ADVENTURES OF HUCKLEBERRY FINN, Mark Twain. (0-486-28061-6)

THE ADVENTURES OF TOM SAWYER, Mark Twain. (0-486-40077-8)

CANDIDE, Voltaire. Edited by Francois-Marie Arouet. (0-486-26689-3)

THE COUNTRY OF THE BLIND: and Other Science-Fiction Stories, H. G. Wells. Edited by Martin Gardner. (0-486-48289-8)

THE WAR OF THE WORLDS, H. G. Wells. (0-486-29506-0)

ETHAN FROME, Edith Wharton. (0-486-26690-7)

THE PICTURE OF DORIAN GRAY, Oscar Wilde. (0-486-27807-7)

MONDAY OR TUESDAY: Eight Stories, Virginia Woolf. (0-486-29453-6)

PLAYS

THE ORESTEIA TRILOGY: Agamemnon, the Libation-Bearers and the Furies, Aeschylus. (0-486-29242-8)

EVERYMAN, Anonymous. (0-486-28726-2)

THE BIRDS, Aristophanes. (0-486-40886-8)

LYSISTRATA, Aristophanes. (0-486-28225-2)

THE CHERRY ORCHARD, Anton Chekhov. (0-486-26682-6)

THE SEA GULL, Anton Chekhov. (0-486-40656-3)

MEDEA, Euripides. (0-486-27548-5)

FAUST, PART ONE, Johann Wolfgang von Goethe. (0-486-28046-2)

THE INSPECTOR GENERAL, Nikolai Gogol. (0-486-28500-6)

SHE STOOPS TO CONQUER, Oliver Goldsmith. (0-486-26867-5)

GHOSTS, Henrik Ibsen. (0-486-29852-3)

A DOLL'S HOUSE, Henrik Ibsen. (0-486-27062-9)

HEDDA GABLER, Henrik Ibsen. (0-486-26469-6)

DR. FAUSTUS, Christopher Marlowe. (0-486-28208-2)

TARTUFFE, Molière. (0-486-41117-6)

BEYOND THE HORIZON, Eugene O'Neill. (0-486-29085-9)

THE EMPEROR JONES, Eugene O'Neill. (0-486-29268-1)

CYRANO DE BERGERAC, Edmond Rostand. (0-486-41119-2)

MEASURE FOR MEASURE: Unabridged, William Shakespeare. (0-486-40889-2)

FOUR GREAT TRAGEDIES: Hamlet, Macbeth, Othello, and Romeo and Juliet, William Shakespeare. (0-486-44083-4)

THE COMEDY OF ERRORS, William Shakespeare. (0-486-42461-8)

HENRY V, William Shakespeare. (0-486-42887-7)

MUCH ADO ABOUT NOTHING, William Shakespeare. (0-486-28272-4)

FIVE GREAT COMEDIES: Much Ado About Nothing, Twelfth Night, A Midsummer Night's Dream, As You Like It and The Merry Wives of Windsor, William Shakespeare. (0-486-44086-9)

OTHELLO, William Shakespeare. (0-486-29097-2)

AS YOU LIKE IT, William Shakespeare. (0-486-40432-3)

ROMEO AND JULIET, William Shakespeare. (0-486-27557-4)

A MIDSUMMER NIGHT'S DREAM, William Shakespeare. (0-486-27067-X)

THE MERCHANT OF VENICE, William Shakespeare. (0-486-28492-1)

HAMLET, William Shakespeare. (0-486-27278-8)

RICHARD III, William Shakespeare. (0-486-28747-5)